J Ocean
Oceanal
Jackpot

$12.95
ocn858895772
11/12/2014

D0403406

ACCOLADES FOR THE
ALDO ZELNICK COMIC NOVEL SERIES

An alphabetical adventure for middle-grade readers 7 to 13

Book of the Year Award, juvenile fiction, *ForeWord Reviews*

Colorado Book Award, juvenile literature

Mountains & Plains Independent Booksellers
Association Regional Book Award

Creative Child magazine Seal of Excellence

Indiebound Kids' Indie Next List selection

Independent Publisher Silver "IPPY" Award

Creative Child magazine Preferred Choice Award

Quid Novi Award, first prize

Moonbeam Children's Book Award,
silver medal for comic/graphic novel

Top 10 Educational Children's Products - Dr. Toy

Book of the Year Award, kids' fiction,
Creative Child magazine

Moonbeam Children's Book Award,
silver medal for activity book

WHAT READERS ARE SAYING:
(kid comments are in Aldo's handwriting)

"It was the funniest book I have ever read.
The illustrations are hilarious. It is better than
Diary of a Wimpy Kid."
— Tavis

"The Aldo Zelnick books keep getting better and better."

— Mary Lee Hahn, teacher and readingyear.blogspot.com blogger

"You will laugh out loud—I guarantee it. The books are THAT funny."

— Becky Bilby, inthepages.blogspot.com

"I've been waiting for a series to come along that could knock Wimpy Kid off its pedestal as the most popular series in my library. Well, this may be it: the Aldo Zelnick Comic Novels. Save room on your shelves for 26 volumes!"
— Donna Dannenmiller, elementary librarian

"Aldo is pretty awesome in my book."

— Dr. Sharon Pajka, English professor, Gallaudet University

"The other night I caught my 8-year-old twins giggling on the living room couch as they took turns reading *Artsy-Fartsy* aloud to each other. Then one morning I found it on their nightstand with a headlamp resting on the cover from the previous night's under-cover reading. That's a true badge of honor in this house. You hit this one out of the park."
— Becky Jensen

"As a teacher of 20 years I have never come across a book that has engaged readers so intensely so quickly. The boys in my reading group devoured the series and were sad when they finished the most recent one."
— Cheryl Weber, Director of Educational Support,
Indian Community School

"One of the most remarkable things about these books is the voice of Aldo, which rings true from every page. The hilarious drawings enhance the text with jokes and visual humor that make Aldo's personality pop."
— Rebecca McGregor, Picture Literacy

"THE BOOK WAS VERY HILARIOUS. IT MADE US LAUGH OUT LOUD. YOU HAVE THE BEST CHARACTERS EVER!"
— Sebastian

"We recommend A is for Aldo! Hilarious stories, goofy drawings, and even sneaky new vocabulary words. If you are an admirer of *Diary of a Wimpy Kid*, you'll adore Aldo Zelnick."
— Oak Park Public Library

"I LOVE the Aldo Zelnick books so much that I want to read them for the rest of my life!"
— Gregory, age 9

"This terrific series will be enjoyed by all readers and constantly in demand. Highly recommended."
— South Sound Book Review Council of Washington libraries

"This is a fun series that my students adore."
— Katherine Sokolowski, 5th grade teacher

"Every library that serves Wimpy Kid fans (which, honestly, is every library, period) should have the Aldo Zelnick series on its shelves."
— Katie Ahearn, children's librarian, Washington DC

"Aldo is an endearing narrator. His deadpan sense of humor is enjoyable even for adults. Each book is a fast-paced, light read, perfect for the kid looking for a transition from comics to chapter books."
— Sarah, children's buyer, Left Bank Books

"When I am reading an Aldo Zelnick book in RTI, I don't want to go back to my classroom. Somehow I want to keep reading...and I don't like reading."
— an elementary student

"I am completely charmed by this series. The drawings and text have the quality of simultaneously being appealing to children and also amusing for adults. A big strength here is in the development of the characters. This is wonderful, since this is going to be an A to Z series and we'll have plenty of time to get to know them better. These are individuals with staying power. With the sketchbook comes a wonderful, not-overstated message of allowing Aldo to be himself and follow his creativity. Bravo!"
— Jean Hanson

"...a must for your elementary school reader."
— Christy, Reader's Cove bookstore

"In the wake of Wimpy Kid and Amelia's Notebooks comes Aldo Zelnick. Oceanak has created a funny and lively hero. The illustrations add to the humor."
— *Library Media Connection*

Jackpot

AN ALDO ZELNICK COMIC NOVEL

Written by Karla Oceanak

Illustrated by Kendra Spanjer

BAILIWICK PRESS

Also by Karla Oceanak and
Kendra Spanjer — Artsy-Fartsy,
Bogus, Cahoots, Dumbstruck,
Egghead, Finicky, Glitch,
Hotdogger, Ignoramus,
All Me, All the Time

This is a work of fiction. Names, characters, places, and incidents are either the product of the author's imagination or are used fictitiously. Any resemblance to actual persons, living or dead, events, or locales is entirely coincidental.

Copyright © 2014 by Karla Oceanak and Kendra Spanjer

All rights reserved. No part of this publication may be reproduced, stored in a retrieval system, or transmitted in any form or by any means, electronic, mechanical, photocopying, or otherwise, without the prior written permission of the publisher.

Published by:
Bailiwick Press
309 East Mulberry Street
Fort Collins, Colorado 80524
(970) 672-4878
Fax: (970) 672-4731
www.bailiwickpress.com
www.aldozelnick.com

Manufactured by:
Bang Printing, Brainerd, Minnesota, USA
March 2014
Job # 1403319

Book design by:
Launie Parry
Red Letter Creative
www.red-letter-creative.com

ISBN 978-1-934649-49-7

Library of Congress Control Number: 2014904467

23 22 21 20 19 18 17 16 15 14   7 6 5 4 3 2 1

Dear Aldo —

Journal* with joy!
Goosy

ALDO,

"In the spring a
young man's fancy
lightly turns to
thoughts of ~~love~~."

— Mr. Mot

FORTUNE
AND
GLORY

WHO'S WHO

ME—
ALDO ZELNICK,
ADVENTURER AND SCHEMER.

MY ROCK-HOUND
FRIENDS, JACK AND
TOMMY.

JOSIE
JEFFERSON,
PALEONTOLOGIST GIRL-LADY.

JACK'S GASSY
DOG, SLATE.

MY FRIEND-
WHO'S-A-GIRL, BEE.

MY FAMILY—TIMOTHY, DAD, AND MOM.

J.D., PAWN SHOP GUY.

JACK'S MOM, MRS. LOPEZ.

MR. MOT, MY BOOKISH NEIGHBOR.

ENCYCLOPEDIA OF JOKES

JACK'S DAD, FRITZ.

BACON BOY, MY OWN COMIC SUPERHERO.

MY GRANDMA, GOOSY.

9

SPRING FEVER

This morning, I said that. I mean, I actually heard my own voice speak those exact words. Me. Aldo Zelnick.

In case you don't know, I pretty much hate OUTSIDE, with all its FRESH AIR and physical activity and lack of cushiony places to sit down. What was I thinking?

It's a Saturday in early March, and I was talking to my best friend, Jack. We were in our fort, which is in my bedroom closet for the winter, because it's too cold here in Colorado for our outside fort underneath a big pine tree in our neighborhood.

Our closet-fort is OK. I mean, it's better than no fort at all, because forts are where kid business happens. For example: Jack and I had spent the whole morning in the closet-fort watching a super-ancient movie called *Raiders of the Lost Ark* on my mom's laptop. Anyways...

"Dude, you just said you want to go OUTSIDE," marveled Jack.

"I know. I must be having a brain attack or something. Let's go find my mom. She'll put her thermometer-hand on my head to see if I'm dying."

(Speech bubble near tree:) PARTY IN THE FORT! ALDO WILL NEVER EVEN KNOW WE WERE HERE...

(Sign:) CLOSED TILL SPRING

We rushed downstairs to the kitchen, where Mom was making bird jewelry* and Dad was stirring a kettle of something red and chunky.

"What's happenin', fellas?" Dad asked. "Pull up a stool and try my irresistible jambalaya.*"

"I don't think I can eat," I said. "Something's wrong with me. See?! I just said I can't eat!"

On cue, Mom palmed my forehead. "You don't have a fever," she frowned. "Do you feel sick?"

"I feel...jittery.*"

"Jittery?"

"Yeah! Like my arms and legs have jumping beans* inside them."

"Aldo," said Dad, putting his hands on my shoulders and bending down to look me straight in the eyeballs...

"Spring fever means your body knows that spring is almost here," said Mom with an amazed grin. "Your arms and legs want to go OUTSIDE, where they can move around! I never thought I'd see this day."

"Weird," I said. "Welp, see ya later, Jack. I'm gonna go take a nap. See if I can sleep off this spring-fever sickness."

But Jack wasn't paying attention to me. Instead, he was standing at the window, looking into my back yard. "It's sunny, and almost all the snow is melted," he noticed. "Let's go check out our fort! Our <u>real</u> fort!"

"Take it easy," I said. "In situations like this, the important thing is not to overreact..."

But Mom was already handing me my boots. "Wear these. It's muddy out there," she said. "Have fun!"

So on this spring-fever day, Jack and my dog, Max, and I trudged down the driveway, across the street, and through the soggy grass field to the giant Colorado Blue Spruce tree where we have our fort. The sky was Smurf-blue, and I could hear real birds twittering, but here and there little blobs of unmelted snow reminded us that winter wasn't 100% gone.

Our feet squished across the wet, brown grass as we got close to our fort tree. But between us and our fort was the ditch. In the summer, it's just a little grassy U that we run through without even thinking about it.

But today the ditch was muddy. Uber muddy.

(ONLY I COULDN'T TELL <u>HOW</u> MUDDY...)

And oops, I hadn't put on my boots like Mom asked me to. I was still wearing my holey shoes. Which, as it turns out, aren't the greatest in mud...

We slip-slided down to the bottom of the ditch, clambered up the far side, and were almost ditch-free when SCHLOOOP...my foot sank into the muck. Actually, my whole right leg disappeared, almost up to my knee. *No big deal,* I thought. *I'll just pull it out.*

So I pushed against the ground with my left leg, trying to tug my right leg from the muddy trap. It didn't budge. I pulled again, this time gritting my teeth and squeezing my eyes shut and asking every jumping-bean muscle in my body to use its spring-fever energy to free me from the abyss of doom, which was about to suck in my whole body and bury me alive.

When that didn't work either, I sorta panicked.

"Help me!" I cried. "Jack, help me! My leg is trapped in quickmud! I can't move! I can't breathe! I can't live! Call 911!"

Jack came running over. "In situations like this, the important thing is not to overreact," he said, tapping his pointer finger on his chin. "This

HOW IT FEELS TO BE STUCK:

TAKE YOUR TIME, GUYS. IT'S NOT LIKE I MIGHT GO EXTINCT OR ANYTHING!!!

TAR PIT

looks like a schist-Gesundheit" (or something like that) "sedimentary formation, so what we probably need to do is..."

If you have a choice, don't pick a rock hound to save you when you are stuck in the earth's crust.

"Just grab me and pull!" I yelled.

So Jack stood behind me, put his arms around my waist, grabbed my belt loops, and pulled with all his scrawny might. And what do you know... Jack's 5th grade muscles must be coming in or something, because my leg started to slide from its muddy tomb...and then, *Pop!* It suctioned out, like a cartoon cork out of a cartoon bottle.

I'M FREEEEEEEEEEEEEEEE!

SAVES THE DAY ONLY TO GET MASHED LIKE A POTATO? JEEPERS*!...

FOOP

And a bunch of mud and rocks and grossness came with Jack and me, all of us sliding down to the bottom of the ditch in a slithery mess.

"We made a mudslide!" said Jack. "Cool!"

"Ughhh. You gave me a monster wedgie."

"Whoa, look at these rocks!" Jack blabbered on. "Check out this one!" And he hoisted a rock the size of a big loaf of bread.

"Yup. That's a big rock all right," I said. "And now that my spring fever is cured, I'm ready to go back inside."

So we walked back to my house, Jack carrying the rock and jabbering* the whole time about geolithic paleontological blah, blah, blah. Mom must've seen us coming, because she ran outside screaming, "Gah! Stop right there!"

BEST. DAY. EVER!

She made us strip down to our undies in the cold garage (*brrr!* and embarrassing!), then she sent Jack to the parent bathroom and me to my bathroom to get clean.

I'm not a big hygiene guy, but I gotta admit, that hot shower felt <u>pretty</u> good.

Afterwards, Jack and I met back up in my bedroom. He was wearing my mom's robe, and his eyes were as round as quarters. He looked like a really surprised, really skinny jaguar.* And he was holding the rock he'd lugged home, only now it was clean. And weird-looking.

"I brought the rock into the shower with me," he whispered. "And it isn't a cool rock after all. It's a cool <u>fossil</u>. And it's not just a cool fossil...I think it might be...a dinosaur bone."

DUDE. I HAVE <u>NEWS</u>.

"Nuh-uh," I scoffed. "Dinosaurs didn't live in our neighborhood."

"Yes, uh-huh!" said Jack. "Dinosaur fossils have been discovered all over Colorado!"

"Really?" That's when an idea jumpstarted* my brain. "Hey! Are dinosaur bones worth something?"

"Dinosaur fossils are priceless!" cried Jack. "They're glimpses into our planet's past! Treasures from ancient history!"

"Not that kind of 'worth something'! I mean, how much could we get for that bone on eBay?"

"Oh!" said Jack, his mouth a cave of surprise. "I don't know. There are a bunch of laws about who fossils belong to and whether or not you can keep them... It depends on who owns the land where the fossils are found..."

"Tell ya what," I said. "Let's keep this bone-rock a secret until we figure out for sure what it is. OK? I'll go get my mom's laptop so you can do some rock-hound research..."

But just then we heard my brother, Timothy, jouncing* down the hallway, toward my room. Real quick I stashed the fossil inside my mountain of a dirty clothes pile.

C'MON YOU GUYS. DINNER. BUT PUT ON SOME REAL CLOTHES FIRST, WOULDJA? GEEZ.

BOND 007

By the time we finished eating (I thought the jambalaya was yumbo, but Jack said he's not ready to eat food with more than 3 ingredients yet, so he had a peanut-butter sandwich), Jack's mom was there to pick him up. So the secret fossil is still wrapped like a mummy inside my used underwear, where it'll be nice and safe until Jack comes back tomorrow and we can figure out just how rich we're gonna be.

JACKPOT*

Jack texted me this morning. I was counting
the organ pipes at the front of the church auditorium
when I felt my leg jiggle.* I thought it was those
spring-fever jumping beans again, but then I realized
it was my phone. I pretended to drop it so I could
crawl under the pew and text Jack back.

After church I excavated the bone from my
dirty-clothes pile, wrapped it in a T-shirt, and
gently placed it into my backpack. Now that Jack
and I are treasure diggers like that Indiana Jones*
guy, I've gotta start taking better care of our
discoveries. I pulled my bike out of the garage and
rode to Jack's house.

Jack's mom, Mrs. Lopez, answered the door. "Hey Mrs. L," I said. "How are things selling on eBay these days?" I bolted past her and up the stairs to Jack's room. Now that you mention it, I forgot to wait for her answer.

Jack was sitting at his desk, gawking at his computer screen. His eyes were red, his face haggard.

"Close the door and let me see it," he said. "<u>Please</u>. I barely got any sleep last night. I've been researching for hours."

Without further ado, I handed him the package. He carefully unwrapped the fossil, smiled joyously,* then gave it a good, long lick.

"Gross!" I said. "Ew! You won't eat jambalaya, but you'll suck on dead dinosaur?!"

Jack's shoulders shrugged, but his face yucked. "I gave it the tongue test. If you lick a rock and your tongue kinda sticks to it, it might be a fossil."

"Oh. Weird. So...did it stick?"

"Maybe a little. Do you have a breath mint?"

I handed him a stick of Juicy Fruit.* "OK. Besides tasting it," I said, "how can you tell if it's a fossil and not just a rock? Cuz, I gotta tell ya, it looks pretty rockish."

UH-OH. IS HE GONNA LICK ME AGAIN?

"It's smooth, filled in with minerals, and has a bony shape," said Jack. "Plus, I found a bunch of dinosaur fossil pictures on the Internet. It looks just like them." He put on his jeweler's glasses* and flicked on their lights. He studied the rock silently for a minute.

"It doesn't look like any rock I've ever inspected," Jack declared, "and I've inspected a lot of rocks. I think we might have to call in an expert."

Hmmm. That sounded really familiar..."Hey!" I remembered. "That's what they always say on that TV show Pawn Store—that they're going to call in an expert! Let's just take it to a pawn shop! Their dinosaur-fossil expert will look it over and bam!—he'll know exactly what it is and how much it's worth!"

"Can kids go to pawn shops?"

"I guess so. As long as we wear our helmets."

So we Googled pawn shops. Conveniently, there was one by the convenience store. We put the fossil back in the backpack and told Mrs. Lopez we were gonna take a bike ride and get Slushies. Which was true. I planned to celebrate our fossil fortune with Slushies and jalapeño* taquitos.

THIS FOSSIL WEIGHS A TON! YOU'LL BE BUYING ME AN EXTRA TAQUITO TO REPLENISH ALL THE EXTRA CALORIES I'M BURNING, DUDE.

THAT FOSSIL WILL BUY US A LIFETIME SUPPLY OF TAQUITOS.

When we got to the pawn store, the first thing I noticed was that it didn't look like the place on the TV show. This one was dinky, and it didn't have cool old stuff for sale, like suits of armor and famous paintings. Mostly it was jam-packed* with boring jewelry, TVs, and guitars.

"What's up, boys?" said the tattooed guy behind the counter.

YES, I'M WEARING A KILT.

"Good day," I said. I knew the pawn jargon.* I would handle this. "We've got a once-in-a-lifetime opportunity for you. An extremely rare and valuable find."

He raised his eyebrows in surprise. "All right... Let's have a look at it!"

"Feast your eyes on...," I said as I set the package on the glass counter and unrolled the bone from its T-shirt wrapper, "a dinosaur fossil."

He chuckled. "Looks like you boys found yourselves a nice rock."

"A rock!" cried Jack. He's usually the calm one, but when you question his rock facts, he can get a little infuriated. "Don't you see?! These Haversian canals are almost completely filled with mineral deposits!"

"Cool your jets,* Jack," I said. "No need to argue. Mister, whaddya say we call in your dinosaur-fossil expert? He'll clear this right up."

This time Pawn Guy didn't just chuckle. He guffawed. "I'm the only expert in this place, kid, and this here's a rock. Customers don't come to my shop to buy boulders, but it <u>would</u> make a good doorstop. I'll give you 2 bucks for it."

Jack's jaw dropped. I calmly rolled up the fossil and returned it to the backpack. Then I reached out my hand to that hirsute, skirt-wearing giant. "I'm sorry we weren't able to come to an agreement," I said as we shook.

As we left, Jack was fuming. "That guy didn't know what he was talking about!"

"I hear you. I hear you," I said. "But the man has a point. If we want maximum value out of this baby, we've gotta think bigger than a pawn shop. What we need is a certificate of

CERTIFICATE OF AUTHENTICITY

Dr. Dino

IT'S AN OFFICIAL-LOOKING PIECE OF PAPER THAT SAYS WHAT SOMETHING IS AND HOW MUCH IT'S WORTH.

authenticity from a grown-up fossil collector. That's what they'd do on *Pawn Store*. Who do you know?"

"Ummm...I can't think of anyone," said Jack. He looked kind of deflated, like a week-old helium balloon.

"OK. Let's sleep on that idea for a day or 2 then. In the meantime, got any Slushie money?"

He did, thank goodness, so even though today didn't turn out to be the day that we got to collect our fortune, at least there were refreshments.

IF THE HAT FITS

On the walk to school this morning, I gave Jack something to make him feel better about the pawn shop episode.

"You are a rock expert," I said. "If you say our fossil is a fossil, then it's a fossil. But not everyone knows how educated you are. So, I was thinking that grown-ups would be more likely to believe us if we looked like paleontologist archeologists." And from my backpack I pulled 2 brown hats. I put one on my head and tossed him the other one.

WHAT WE NEED TO GO WITH THESE HATS ARE MOUSTACHES. AND STUBBLE. DO I HAVE ANY STUBBLE COMING IN?

NO, BUT MY COUSINS IN MEXICO SAY I COULD GET MY MOUSTACHE ANY DAY NOW.

"Whoa! Where'd ya get these?" asked Jack.

"My dad went through a hat-wearing phase in the 80s. Anyways, last night I asked him about Indiana Jones, and he dug these out of his closet."

"You didn't tell him about the fossil, did you?"

"Nah. It'll be more fun to surprise our families with a chest full of hundred-dollar bills. Maybe we can finally go to Disney World..."

DOES THIS MEAN I HAVE TO START BEING NICE TO ALDO?

"Hey," said Jack. "I thought of someone who might be able to identify the fossil and make us a certificate of authenticity."

"Excellent!" I said. "Who?"

"This lady paleontologist at the Museum of Natural History in Boulder. My mom took me there for Kids Day once, and the lady showed us dinosaur bones. Maybe we can go there next weekend."

"Perfect."

"OK. I'll ask my mom tonight."

I looked over and saw that Jack was smiling. His step seemed jauntier* too. "So what are you gonna do with your half of the fortune?" I asked.

"I dunno. It'd be sweet to have a dinosaur named after me. They do that sometimes, when you discover a kind that no one's ever found before."

"Jackosaurus. I'm down with that. But Aldozelnidon sounds pretty legit too..."

"If I can have the name, you can have some of my half of the jackpot," Jack offered.

"Hm. Swapping fortune for glory. You'd be the star; I'd be the money man. Sounds like a good partnership."

We shook on it. When we swaggered onto the Dana Elementary playground, the place went silent. All the kids froze mid-chaos and stared at us in our awesome hattedness. We just touched the brims in silent greeting and kept on walking.

p.s. In case you're wondering, the Jackosaurus fossil is now safe inside a locked case under Jack's bed in his bedroom. Even undie-mummies are risky hiding spots when laundry day rolls around.

SO...HOW MUCH?

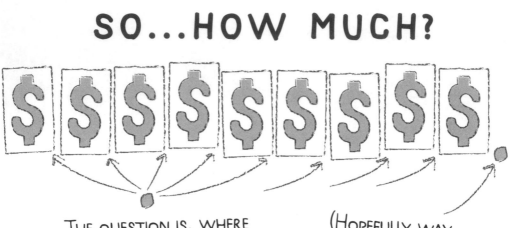

THE QUESTION IS, WHERE WILL THE DECIMAL POINT GO?

(HOPEFULLY WAY OVER HERE!)

Jack and I broke off from the handball game at lunch recess today so I could ask him The Question that had been doing jumping jacks* in my head at school all morning, making it mega hard to concentrate during Spanish, Grammar, Language Arts, and Band.

"I've been wondering," I whispered, "just how much money we might be talking about. You did all that fossil research, but this morning I realized, right in the middle of Señor Espinoza making us practice pronouncing our Spanish Js like Hs...which is weird because why don't you just start all those J words with an H?...that I never heard you say a number. What is our Jackosaurus bone worth?"

"It's hard to say," whispered Jack, "but I did read a true story about a T. rex named Sue. She was found in South Dakota, and someone bought her bones at an auction for 7-and-a-half <u>million</u> dollars."

I gave a long, low whistle and tipped my Indy hat back a little farther on my head.

"I know," smiled Jack. "That was for an entire skeleton. But here's what I've been thinking: If one dinosaur bone was hiding in our ditch, there are probably others."

WELL DON'T JUST STAND THERE!!! LET'S GET DIGGING!

"FREEZE, ALDO!" Jack hollered after me. "We <u>can't</u> just go digging around in that ditch! That would wreck the integrity of the site!"

"What does 'integrity of the site' mean?"

"It means that there's a right way to excavate fossils, and there's a wrong way. If you find a big animal fossil buried in the ground, you're not supposed to dig it up. That's one of the main rules of rock hounding— I could lose my badge over that! What you're supposed to do is tell a paleontologist, so the pros can check it out."

"But we didn't dig up Jackosaurus. The ground burped him out!"

"Right," confirmed Jack. "So we're OK. But we're probably not gonna get rich and famous from just the one bone. It's the rest of the skeleton still hiding under the ground that could bring us fortune and glory. IF we do things right."

"You're saying it's like we found a key to a treasure chest!" I announced a little too loudly. "We can show the key to an expert, but we're the only ones who know where the chest is buried!"

"You guys found buried treasure?" said a voice behind us. It was Bee! She's homeschooled, but she comes to Dana Elementary for certain classes.

SHE'S OUR FRIEND AND ALL, BUT FINDERS KEEPERS, AM I RIGHT? FORTUNE CAN ONLY BE SPLIT SO MANY WAYS BEFORE IT'S NOT A FORTUNE ANYMORE.

THIS GIRL IS A JUGGERNAUT* OF CURIOSITY.

"Oh...heh...that's...just an expression," I said. "So...how 'bout that Jell-o at lunch? It was a little more jiggly today than usual, didn't you think?"

Bee didn't ask any more questions, but I could tell from the dubious scrunch of her eyes that she wasn't satisfied by my answer.

JOURNALISM 101

    Jack and I have been rocking our Indiana
Jones hats for 3 days now. We're not allowed to
wear them in Mr. Krug's room (he's our 5th grade
teacher), so during class time we stash them in our
lockers. But we go Indy-style for lunch recess, and
of course, we wear them before and after school.

    I've noticed that our hat-wearing is starting to
cause a kerfuffle. (My word-nerd neighbor, Mr. Mot,
told me that word today. It means a commotion
or hubbub. *Hmmm...it's an excellent K word...*)

For example, my brother, Timothy, is jealous*
of me! This morning I was wearing my hat
at breakfast as I read my mom's *Smithsonian*
magazine, and he reached over and flicked it off my
head.

"Just because you're wearing a cool hat
doesn't mean you're cool," he blurted.

"It's the other way around, actually," I said
as I coolly picked up the hat and settled it back
atop my head. "I'm cool, so naturally I wear a cool
hat."

"He looks pretty cool to me," said Mom.
"But I do wonder what he's up to..."

"Just because I'm wearing a hat doesn't mean
I'm up to something!" I said, not so coolly, and I
huffed out of the kitchen before she could cook up
any more questions.

Then right after school, I got a text from Bee:

Extra pizza. My house. You and
Jack hungry? (I know YOU are...)

Politely, I waited until after Bee had handed
me some pizza to bring up the copycat thing.
"You're not the first person to notice how alluring
Jack and I look in these hats," I said. "But that
doesn't mean you should start wearing one too."

"My hat doesn't have anything to do with yours," said Bee. "I'm learning about journalism* this month in homeschool. I might want to become a journalist, and this is the kind of hat journalists wear. But now that you mention it, I think I <u>will</u> interview you about your hats." And she held a pen to her pad of paper as she said, "So, Mr. Zelnick, you and Mr. Jack Lopez have been seen wearing matching brown hats for several days in a row now. What is the reason for this unusual case of head covering?"

This wasn't just pizza generosity. This was a trap! Jack and I looked at each other. His eyes got big, and he stuffed a fat wad of pizza into his mouth to keep himself from saying something he shouldn't.

Me, I wasn't about to be shaken by a few nosy questions. "Oh, Jack and I have simply become Indiana Jones enthusiasts," I said. "Are you familiar with his work?"

MFFF!

45

Bee scribbled on her notepad then looked back up at me. "I'll ask the questions around here," she said. "In my interview with Mrs. Lopez, I also learned that the 2 of you were overheard discussing bones and pawn shops."

WOULD YOU CARE TO COMMENT?

Jack took another jumbo* bite of pizza. I tugged at my shirt collar. It was starting to feel a little bit hot there in Bee's kitchen.

"Oh, you know Jack," I said. "Every other word that comes out of his mouth is 'rock' this or 'fossil' that."

I DIDN'T MENTION THE WORD 'FOSSIL.'

Bee grinned her smarty-pants grin. "Did the two of you find a fossil? How? When? Where? What kind?"

Jack stood and turned to leave. "Zhrarasawazza," he said through a mouthful of chewed-up cheese as he ran out the door.

I SEE...IS THAT A 'NO COMMENT'?

I looked at Bee in her journalist hat and journalist smirk and *bam!*, came up with an Indiana Jones-cagey idea for escaping this line of questioning. "Off the record?" I asked.

Bee frowned, but after a couple of seconds she set down her notepad and pen.

"Off the record," I continued, "the pawn-shop guy said it's a rock. End of story. Now, you got any more pepperoni?"

My answer seemed to satisfy Bee for now—and I didn't even have to lie to her. But Jack and I had better cash in on our dino jackpot before Bee lets the Jackosaurus out of the bag, er...ditch.

SUCH A GENUS

Q. WHY CAN'T YOU HEAR A PTERANODON USING THE BATHROOM? (MOST OF THE TIME.)

MOOOM!!! I NEED HELP WITH THE TOILET PAPER AGAIN!!!

A. BECAUSE THE "p" IS SILENT.

After school today Jack and I stopped by Mr. Mot's to see if he had any dinosaur books in his library. I mean, Wikipedia's great and everything, but sometimes you just need to hold words and pictures in your hands to know that they represent things that are real.

"Are you boys studying the fossil record in school?" asked Mr. Mot as Jack and I looked through the stack of dinosaur books he pulled off his shelves for us.

"Nah, we're just doing a little independent study," I explained. "You know, pursuing our interests to enhance our educational experience."

"Righhht...," said Mr. Mot.

"Hey, I think I checked this book out from the library-library when I was a kid!" I said, holding up the *Encyclopedia of Dinosaurs*. "It's got illustrations of every kind of dinosaur and tells all about them!"

"Oh I love that book!" cried Jack, and he grabbed it from me and hugged it to his chest.

Mr. Mot went to make us a snack while Jack and I sprawled on the floor and flipped through the encyclopedia together.

"I forgot there were so many kinds of dinosaurs," I whispered. "Geez, how are we ever gonna figure out which kind we found?"

THE ONLY THING JACK LOVES MORE THAN ROCKS AND FOSSILS ARE BOOKS ABOUT ROCKS AND FOSSILS.

"I know," Jack whispered back. "We definitely need help identifying the genus. By the way, my mom said she'd take us to the natural history museum on Saturday."

"Yesss! Wait, I thought <u>you</u> were the genius."

"<u>Genus</u>, not genius. Genus means the type. Like, Tyrannosaurus is a genus of dinosaur."

"Whoa. What if our Jackosaurus is a T. rex? That would mean T. rexes hunted in our backyards!"

WHO WANTS TAQUITOS WHEN YOU CAN HAVE HOMBRECITOS!

WHAT BIG TEETH YOU HAVE!

EAT ALDO! I'VE GOT NO MEAT ON MY BONES!

"T. rexes <u>have</u> been discovered in...," Jack started to say, but he stopped because just then Mr. Mot carried in a bowl of small, white sticks in one hand and in the other, another book.

"For your hunger for sustenance, I bring julienned* jicama,*" said Mr. Mot. "For your hunger for Jurassic* vertebrates, I bring a classic—Journey to the Center of the Earth, by Jules Verne."

(You've gotta love Mr. Mot. Too bad he's so old. He can't have that many good years left.)

I'M 70 YEARS YOUNG!

I'M 70 TOO—70 MILLION.

Anyways, Mr. Mot said we could borrow whichever books we wanted, so I zipped the dino encyclopedia and the Journey book into my backpack. We were just leaving his house when who popped out from behind his bushes but Miss B. Journalist (the B. must be for busybody).

"Doing some research in Mr. Mot's library, are we?" she asked.

"Just having a healthy after-school snack! Jicama! It's a vegetable! Ever heard of it?" I called as I jogged* to my house. Jack took off like a jackrabbit* in the direction of his. Geez. That girl's too smart for our own good.

TYRANNONINJA

(TURN THE PAGE)

"CREATIVITY IS JUST CONNECTING THINGS."
— STEVE JOBS* ↰ MY GRANDMA GOOSY TOLD ME THIS.

Since it's a school night, I'm supposed to be sleeping by now, but an audacious idea just boinged me right out of bed.

I'm a cartoonist, right? And I'm about to be a famous dinosaur discoverer, right? So obviously, I should also invent a team of dinosaur cartoon characters! How cool would that be? Also, I'd have two sources of fortune and glory—1. Our Jackosaurus fossil; and 2. My dinosaur superheroes!

So, here goes. Here's my first Dino Hero.

"TYRANNO" MEANS TYRANT. "NINJA" IS A SMART, SPEEDY, AND SUPER-COORDINATED JAPANESE WARRIOR. MASH THEM TOGETHER AND YOU'VE GOT A DEADLY COMBINATION OF POWER, SPEED, SNEAKINESS, AND BRAINS.

TEMPLE OF DOOM

It's Friday night. Jack and I just watched *Indiana Jones and the Temple of Doom*. It's the second Indiana Jones movie, and it's so ancient (1984!) that the only place Mrs. Lopez could find it for us was at the public library.

"What's this?" Jack asked his mom when she handed him the big plastic rectangle.

IT'S CALLED A VHS TAPE. IT'S HOW MOVIES WERE PACKAGED BEFORE DVDs AND STREAMING.

WHAT DOES VHS STAND FOR, ANYWAY?

VERY HUMONGOUS SIZE?

In the movie, Indy saves a bunch of kids from slavery by rescuing a lucky rock from a bad guy. Then Indy returns the rock and the kids to their village, and everyone loves him.

"See! Rocks rule!" said Jack.

"Indiana Jones rules," I said. "Except...I've noticed that whenever he risks his life to find a valuable rock or treasure of some kind, he gets glory...but no fortune. What's up with that?"

I'm sleeping over at Jack's tonight so we can get up and go to the natural history museum first thing in the morning. That means tomorrow is the day Jack and I get rich and famous!

I figure they won't just want to give us a certificate of authenticity. They'll want to buy the skeleton immediately! I wonder how it will work. Do museums have a big vault of money just sitting there...and when you walk in with an important artifact, a security guard unlocks the vault, grabs a bag of money, and gives it to you in exchange for the treasure?

Jack and I prepared our museum backpack tonight. It contains the fossil, wrapped in a towel; Jack's jeweler's glasses; a notebook with some notes Jack wrote; a pencil; and Junior Mints in case all that jackpot-hitting makes us hungry.

"Do you think we should let your mom in on the fossil, since she's the one taking us to the museum tomorrow?" I asked as we lay there in our jammies,* too jazzed* to fall asleep.

"Yeah, we should probably tell her we found something we want to show to the paleontologist," Jack said. "Plus, I'm not sure the museum people will hand <u>us</u> the money, since we're kids. We might need her momness."

"OK. Let's talk to her in the morning."

"Sounds good." Jack yawned then added, "Hey, do you think our lives will get weird when we're rich and famous? Cuz...I like my life the way it is."

I leaned down from the top bunk to check Jack's face. I needed to see if he was kidding. It didn't <u>sound</u> like he was kidding. But his expression was hidden in the shadows.

"Just imagine our same lives," I said, "only with better accessories. Like better phones...and new video games...and bikes with motors, so we don't have to pedal. And maybe a coupla trips somewhere awesome each year."

"But...," Jack paused. I could tell he was thinking about how to put the right words together. "Like, what if your family decided to spend the money on a fancier house...in a fancier neighborhood? That would be...dumb."

I hadn't thought of that. I didn't like the idea of one of us moving away any more than he did. "Nah...we'll keep it real," I reassured him. "I know! Let's make a promise right now and write it down in my sketchbook. That way, if one of us lets fortune and glory go to his head, the other one can show him the oath, to un-brainwash him."

DECLARATION OF NORMALNESS

WE, ALDO ZELNICK AND JACK LOPEZ, HOLD THESE TRUTHS TO BE SELF-EXCELLENT. AFTER WE BECOME RICH AND FAMOUS FROM SELLING OUR MEGA-VALUABLE JACKOSAURUS FOSSIL, WE WILL STILL BE YOUR BASIC NICE GUYS WHO LIVE THE SIMPLE LIFE AND DON'T THINK WE'RE BETTER THAN OTHER PEOPLE JUST BECAUSE WE MADE ONE OF THE MOST IMPORTANT DISCOVERIES IN THE HISTORY OF CIVILIZATION.

WHEN WE SAY "THE SIMPLE LIFE," WE DON'T MEAN AMISH-STYLE. WE'LL USE ELECTRICITY AND RIDE IN CARS AND TAKE HOT SHOWERS ONCE IN A WHILE ETC., BUT EVEN THOUGH WE'LL BUY SOME COOL STUFF, WE WON'T ACT ALL RICHY-RICH AND LIVE IN FANCY HOUSES, BECAUSE WE'RE CHILL LIKE THAT. WE'LL PROBABLY STAY IN THE JACKALOPE JUNCTION NEIGHBORHOOD FOREVER.

SIGNED,

Aldo Zelnick

Jack Lopez

P.S. IN CASE YOU DIDN'T KNOW...
JACKALOPE = JACKRABBIT + ANTELOPE
IT'S A MYTHICAL CREATURE OF THE AMERICAN WEST.

I MAY LOOK LIKE A CUDDLY BUNNY, BUT I'VE GOT HORNS! YOU WANNA GO?

The Declaration seemed to help Jack rest easier, cuz he's asleep now. I stayed up a little bit longer to get all this down on paper. It's heavenly knowing that tomorrow night at this time I'll probably be a millionaire. But I guess even millionaires need shut-eye, so...

...I'LL JUST CATCH SOME Zs ON CLOUD 9 MILLION.

DAY AT THE MUSEUM

The morning started out with Jack's mom calling us to breakfast. While we sipped *jugo de naranja** and devoured *jamon-y-huevos** burritos, we finally leaked our fossil secret to someone else.

"Ya see, we got caught in a mudslide, in the ditch by our fort," I explained to Mrs. Lopez. "Don't worry, I'm OK. Just a little banged up. Anyways, the mudslide spit out some rocks from the top of the ditch."

"So then I brought one of the rocks to Aldo's house," said Jack.

"Of course," nodded Mrs. Lopez.

"And after I washed it off," he continued, "I realized it wasn't a rock—it was a fossil!"

"That's when he licked it," I added.

"So then I did some research," said Jack, "and I'm pretty sure it's a <u>dinosaur</u> fossil. But we need the museum experts to confirm my findings and tell us the genus."

"And give us the money. Don't forget about the money," I added.

"What money?" Mrs. Lopez asked.

That's when the doorbell rang.

DING-DONG!

"Oh! That's probably Tommy," said Mrs. Lopez as she went to the door, and before Jack and I could say anything, in walked our friend and fellow rock fanatic, Tommy Geller.

HEY GUYS! DID YOU HEAR WHY THERE ARE OLD DINOSAUR BONES IN THIS MUSEUM?

BECAUSE THEY CAN'T FIND ANY <u>NEW</u> ONES! AHAHAHA. GET IT?

ROCK-HOUND HUMOR. SHEESH.

"I forgot to tell you boys that I invited Tommy to come to the museum with us," said Mrs. Lopez. "I saw him on my walk yesterday and remembered how much he likes rocks and fossils too. So, what were you saying about money, Aldo?"

"Oh...I uh...I was just thinking...that I uh... forgot to bring money to get into the museum."

"It's free, silly!" said Mrs. Lopez. "Should we get going?"

Now we're on the one-hour car ride to the museum. Tommy is jabbering with Mrs. Lopez, Jack's studying the dino encyclopedia and guarding the Jackosaurus backpack on the floor between his feet, and me, I'm doing this—writing in my sketchbook.

What if we <u>did</u> split our 7-and-a-half million dollars 3 ways? I mean, we wouldn't <u>have</u> to give Tommy a share, but since he's here, I suppose we could...

MATH BREAK:

So that's 2-and-a-half million each if we shared it equally. But Tommy didn't <u>discover</u> the Jackosaurus, so he'd probably be all happy with a million or so. Yeah, I think Jack and I can cut him in. Cuz like we said, we're your basic nice guys. And also, <u>not</u> sharing might be bad juju.*

$$\overset{\displaystyle\boxed{\$2,500,000}}{3\overline{)\$7,500,000}}$$

$$
\begin{array}{r}
-6 \quad\quad\quad\quad\quad\quad 3\times2 = 6 \\
15 \quad\quad\quad\quad\quad\quad \\
-15 \quad\quad\quad\quad 3\times5 = 15 \\
00 \quad\quad\quad\quad \\
-0 \quad\quad\quad\quad 3\times0 = 0 \\
00 \quad\quad\quad \\
-0 \quad\quad\quad 3\times0 = 0 \\
0,0 \quad\quad \\
-0 \quad\quad 3\times0 = 0 \\
00 \quad\quad \\
-0 \quad 3\times0 = 0 \\
00 \quad \\
-0 \quad 3\times0 = 0 \\
0
\end{array}
$$

Ope! We're at the museum already! Catch you on the flip side.

(I JUST REALIZED THAT WHEN I COME BACK, IT'LL BE ON THE <u>FLIP SIDE</u> OF THIS PIECE OF PAPER TOO! AWESOME!)

Welp, we're back in the car, on the way home from the museum. I thought we'd be building a back-seat fort with fat stacks of hundred-dollar bills by now...

...but instead we got jack squat.* They didn't even give us a measly certificate of authenticity. *Gah!*

Here's what happened:

Indy-style, we walked up to the museum building and jauntily swung open the heavy black doors. Jack led us up the stairs, to the right, and into the dinosaur room.

"Where are all the giant skeletons?" I asked immediately. I mean, there were random bones and small skeletons in glass cases, but no T. rex types, if you know what I'm sayin'.

"They don't have big dinosaurs," said Jack, who had that jubilant,* trance-y look on face he gets whenever he's surrounded by stuff found below the ground. "At least, not entire skeletons. They have some really cool pieces though." He walked over to a jumbo skull. "See. This is a Triceratops. Isn't he handsome?"

TRICERATOPS
HORRIDUS

"Ah geez. Don't kiss him," I said. "So, how much do you think they paid for Mr. Triceratops?"

"That's a good question," said a new voice. "This skull was discovered by one of the first U.S. government paleontologists, in 1891. So from the beginning, this Triceratops belonged to the public."

I turned to see a girl-lady with short brown hair. Her nametag said Josie Jefferson, Graduate Assistant, Department of Paleontology.

FUN FACT: THE FIRST TRICERATOPS EVER DISCOVERED WAS FOUND IN COLORADO.

"Hi," said Jack's mom. "I'm Jovana Lopez.

SEE! THAT'S ONE OF THOSE SPANISH J WORDS THAT SOUNDS LIKE IT STARTS WITH H!

This is my son, Jack, and his friends Aldo and Tommy.

They're way into dinosaurs these days."

"Nice to meet you," said Josie. "I'm way into dinosaurs myself."

"Well, we came here because we found something," said Jack shyly. "We brought it to show to an expert. Would you look at it?"

"Sure," said Josie. "I'm just learning to be a paleontologist, but I know a few things."

Jack set his backpack on a bench, got out the Jackosaurus, and handed it to Josie. "I think it's a dinosaur bone," he said. "The guy at the pawn shop said it's just a rock, but I'm a rock collector. It sure looks like a fossil to me."

Josie sat on the bench and turned the fossil over in her hands. She looked at the sides. She inspected the ends. She petted it like it was a kitten. I held my breath and watched her. Inside her expert skull was an expert brain slowly and carefully making expert calculations that could make the difference between me getting enough money to buy a Hawaiian vacation condo (like the one Mr. Mot's brother has)...or a Hawaiian shirt.

"It's an exceedingly rare specimen," Josie said at last. "Would you take 10 million dollars for it?"

YESSS!!!

But when everyone stared at me, I realized that Josie had only said that in my <u>imagination.</u>

"I mean...'Yes, I think it looks pretty fossily too,'" I said, hoping I hadn't just jinxed* everything.

After another infinite pause, Josie actually did speak. "Wow, Jack, this really might be a dinosaur bone. You're right...it's still shaped like a bone, but special conditions and millions of years have changed it into something extraordinary—not really a bone, but not really an ordinary rock either. As a bone slooowly becomes a fossil, some minerals take the place of bone cells, and others fill in the bone's tiny holes. Over time, the bone becomes more and more rock-like. That's why fossils can be mistaken for regular rocks."

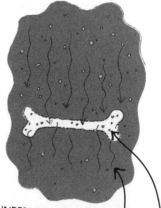

IN UNDERGROUND MUD, WATER CARRIES MINERALS. THE WATER CAN PASS THROUGH A BURIED BONE, BUT SOME OF THE MINERALS GET STUCK!

"As for what animal it might have belonged to? I don't know," Josie admitted. "It's too big to be a prehistoric bird or a scaled reptile, and it looks much too old to be a mammal. Where did you find it?"

"In our neighborhood," said Jack.

"Where, exactly, in your neighborhood? Someone's yard?" Josie asked.

"No, it was in a muddy ditch, in a field by my house," I said. "Close to our fort."

"And where do you live?"

"In Fort Collins," said Tommy.

"Hmmm...," she said. "I'm not sure that jibes.* I'll have to check the geological-survey maps, but I think most of Fort Collins sits on top of ancient river deposits and Late Cretaceous—"

"Wait a sec," I interjected. "Isn't that like, shellfish? Crabs are Cretaceous, right? Why would anyone build a town on top of crabs? But I do like crabcakes..."

"Crabs are crustaceous," said Mrs. Lopez. "Cretaceous is a geological period."

Josie whipped out a notebook and made us this drawing:

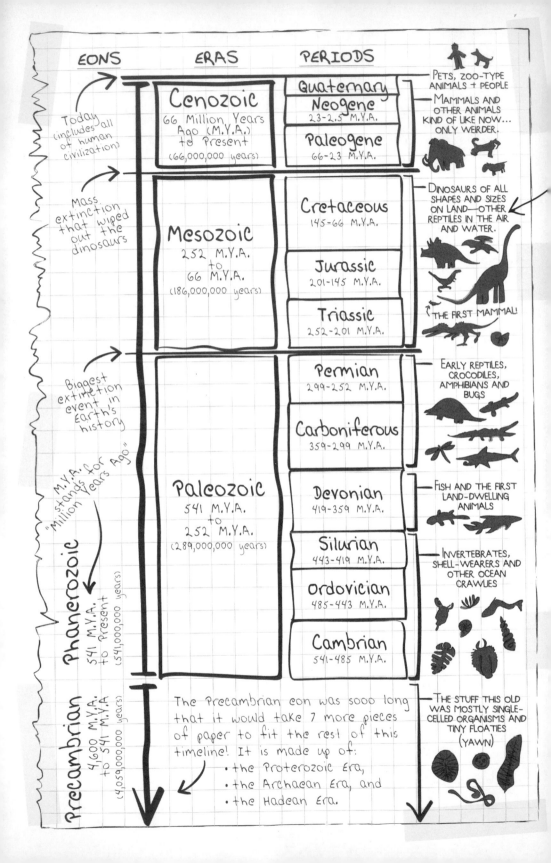

EONS | ERAS | PERIODS

Cenozoic 66 Million Years Ago (M.Y.A.) to Present (66,000,000 years)
- Quaternary
- Neogene 23-2.5 M.Y.A.
- Paleogene 66-23 M.Y.A.

Today (includes all of human civilization)

PETS, ZOO-TYPE ANIMALS + PEOPLE

MAMMALS AND OTHER ANIMALS KIND OF LIKE NOW... ONLY WEIRDER.

Mass extinction that wiped out the dinosaurs

Mesozoic 252 M.Y.A. to 66 M.Y.A. (186,000,000 years)
- Cretaceous 145-66 M.Y.A.
- Jurassic 201-145 M.Y.A.
- Triassic 252-201 M.Y.A.

DINOSAURS OF ALL SHAPES AND SIZES ON LAND—OTHER REPTILES IN THE AIR AND WATER.

THE FIRST MAMMAL!

Biggest extinction event in Earth's history

M.Y.A. stands for "Million Years Ago"

Paleozoic 541 M.Y.A. to 252 M.Y.A. (289,000,000 years)
- Permian 299-252 M.Y.A.
- Carboniferous 359-299 M.Y.A.
- Devonian 419-359 M.Y.A.
- Silurian 443-419 M.Y.A.
- Ordovician 485-443 M.Y.A.
- Cambrian 541-485 M.Y.A.

EARLY REPTILES, CROCODILES, AMPHIBIANS AND BUGS

FISH AND THE FIRST LAND-DWELLING ANIMALS

INVERTEBRATES, SHELL-WEARERS AND OTHER OCEAN CRAWLIES

Phanerozoic 541 M.Y.A. to Present (541,000,000 years)

Precambrian 4,600 M.Y.A. to 541 M.Y.A. (4,059,000,000 years)

The Precambrian eon was sooo long that it would take 7 more pieces of paper to fit the rest of this timeline! It is made up of:
- the Proterozoic Era,
- the Archaean Era, and
- the Hadean Era.

THE STUFF THIS OLD WAS MOSTLY SINGLE-CELLED ORGANISMS AND TINY FLOATIES (YAWN)

SO, IF THIS BONE CAME OUT OF A CRETACEOUS FORMATION, THEN THERE'S A GOOD CHANCE IT'S A CRETACEOUS DINOSAUR.

BUT IF THE CRETACEOUS PERIOD WAS ALMOST 80 MILLION YEARS LONG, THERE MUST HAVE BEEN JILLIONS* OF DIFFERENT ANIMALS ALIVE DURING THAT TIME. HOW ARE WE EVER GOING TO FIGURE OUT WHICH DINOSAUR THIS ONE BONE CAME FROM?

THAT'S NOT THE ONLY PROBLEM. I CAN'T EVEN BE SURE IT'S CRETACEOUS UNTIL I SEE THE ROCK IT CAME FROM. THIS BONE'S OWNER COULD HAVE LIVED ANY TIME DURING THE MESOZOIC ERA—THE AGE OF REPTILES—WHICH LASTED 186 MILLION YEARS.

"OK, OK," I said. "That's enough talk about how many millions of years. What I really want to know is: How many millions of dollars? We've got a piece of a dinosaur, and since everyone knows that a leg bone connects to a hip bone, etcetera, there's probably a whole skeleton in that ditch, just dying to get discovered. So if you'll direct us to your Fortune-and-Glory counter, we're ready to sell our fossil and location information."

73

Josie smiled. I could tell right away it wasn't a fortune-and-glory smile.

"Unfortunately, this museum doesn't have millions of dollars to buy fossils," said Josie.

"That's dumb," I muttered.

BUT MAKING A SCIENTIFIC DISCOVERY <u>FEELS</u> LIKE WINNING THE LOTTERY, DOESN'T IT?

WINK!

HM. I WOULDN'T KNOW, BUT SOMEHOW I DOUBT IT.

"Boys, we have a long way to go before we can identify the species," said Josie. "Judging from its shape, size, and structure, I'd say this bone belonged to a large land animal. Our best clues will be found at the site—but before we even <u>think</u> about digging, we need to find out who owns the ditch and the field. We can't go look for the rest of the skeleton until we know it's OK with the owners."

"I think the neighborhood owns that land," said Mrs. Lopez. "I'm on the home owners' association board, so I can find out."

"Wait a sec!" I said. "Are you saying that <u>all</u> of the families who live in Jackalope Junction own Jackosaurus?"

"It's possible," said Mrs. Lopez.

"Sweet," said Tommy-the-Interloper.

"But...what about the ownership law that everybody <u>actually</u> follows: finders keepers?" I asked.

"Let's take this one step at a time," said Mrs. Lopez. "It sounds like we have some research to do before we worry about who owns a dinosaur skeleton that might not even exist."

"Thanks for taking such good care of the fossil, Jack," said Josie as we got ready to leave. "I can tell that you're an excellent scientist—and a responsible one too. This dinosaur could be an important find. I'm happy to know it's in your capable hands."

Jack's skinny chest puffed up so big with proudness that his Junior Geologists Society badge practically popped off.

Mrs. Lopez and Josie swapped e-mail addresses and phone numbers, and Josie said she might come to Jackalope Junction in a few days to check out the fossil ditch.

Hm. If Josie was telling the truth and the museum <u>doesn't</u> have millions of dollars to buy Jackosaurus, maybe someone on eBay does. Still, a lot of people live in our neighborhood—200 families, let's say—and if we have to split the jackpot with all of them, even 7-and-a-half million doesn't go that far...

WHAT CAN YOU POSSIBLY BUY WITH $37,500 THESE DAYS?

$$
\begin{array}{r}
\left(\$0\,0\,3\,7{,}5\,0\,0\right) \\
200\overline{)\,\$7{,}500{,}000} \\
\end{array}
$$

```
        ( $0 0 37,500 )
  200) $7,500,000
      -0              200x0 = 0
       7 5
      - 0             200x0 = 0
       750
      -600            200x3 = 600
       1500
      -1400           200x7 = 1400
       1000
      -1000           200x5 = 1000
        00
       - 0            200x0 = 0
        00
       - 0            200x0 = 0
        0
```

DITCHED

THIS IS WHERE WE FOUND THE BONE. WHAT ELSE COULD BE DOWN THERE?!

After Jack and Tommy and I got back home from the museum, we went straight to the fossil ditch to see if any more skeleton pieces happened to be poking out.

"We <u>cannot</u> dig," emphasized Jack. "But we can look. With just our eyes. OK?"

It was another warm spring Saturday, and the ditch was even muddier than last week. But we slip-slided down into it anyways, on the side across from the fossil pit, cuz paleontologist treasure-hunters like us don't think twice about getting our hands—well basically our whole bodies—dirty.

"Right here is where I almost lost my right leg," I showed Tommy. "But that was a price I was willing to pay for fortune and glory."

"I don't see anything that looks like a fossil," Tommy said. He and Jack had locked their eyes about an inch from the ditch wall and were moving their heads back and forth. "Are you sure this is the right spot?"

"Did velociraptor have feathers?!" answered Jack.

"That's du...," I started to say, because if you've seen the movie *Jurassic Park*, you know that velociraptors were some of the fiercest dinosaurs in the universe, and you can't juxtapose* fierceness and feathers, but Tommy cut me off.

"Shhh...," he whispered. "Get down!"

We hunkered into the muddy corner of the ditch. A man's voice was approaching.

"So they found it somewhere along the bank," he was saying. "But we don't know exactly where? Right. OK."

Jack gave me the universal "phone call" signal, and I nodded. The guy was talking on his cell phone. It wasn't a voice I knew well, yet it sounded familiar somehow. And it kept getting closer...and closer...

By now the voice was right behind us. We had smooshed ourselves so far into the muck that we were practically planted, like human beans.

"Well, I don't see anything," he said. "But if fortune and glory are involved, we'd better find it." He laughed a deep, throaty laugh. "Millions? Oh yes. We could use millions." His voice began to grow fainter. He was leaving! But the final thing we heard him say was as clear as a bell: "I guess I should've gotten it from them when I had the chance."

I peered over the top of the ditch to see a hulk of a man lumbering away, still with his phone to his ear. I ducked back down.

"That was the pawn shop dude!" I whispered. "J.D.!"

"I knew I should have busted out my jujitsu* moves on that guy!" hissed Jack.

"So...," I thought out loud. "He must've known it was a valuable fossil this whole time! I bet he's gonna figure out where the skeleton is, dig it up in the middle of the night, and sell it!"

"Who was he talking to?" wondered Tommy.

"This is just like Indiana Jones!" I said. "There's always a whole <u>team</u> of bad guys. He was talking to the head honcho bad guy!"

Jack's face looked as serious as a Monday without pizza for lunch. "We'd better tell my mom and call Josie," he said, "We need to let her know the site is in danger."

MOST OF THE TIME JACK'S THE MOST JOVIAL* KID I KNOW, BUT IF YOU MESS WITH HIS ROCKS, WATCH OUT! HE'LL GO ALL JEKYLL-AND-HYDE* ON YOU.

ROCKS ARE NEAT! FRIENDS ARE AWESOME!

BACK AWAY FROM THE HISTORICAL ARTIFACT AND NO ONE GETS HURT!

BACK AT JACK'S

We ran to Jack's mom-house. By the time I got there, Jack and Tommy were already in the middle of telling Mrs. Lopez about what happened.

YOU WOULDN'T KNOW IT TO LOOK AT HIM, BUT TOMMY RUNS JUST AS FAST AS JACK.

THIS IS NO TIME TO JUDGE A JOGGER BY THE SIZE OF HIS JEANS!

"...And the bad guy was wearing a kilt!" I gasped, sucking in big lungfuls of air. "He looks kind of like Hagrid"...gasp, gasp..."in a man-skirt!"

"Does he have tattoos on his arms?" asked Mrs. Lopez.

"Yes!" said Jack. "And he works at the pawn shop!"

"That's Mr. Dean!" said Mrs. Lopez. "He lives in Jackalope Junction too. And guess who he was talking to on the phone? Me! He's on the home owners' association board too. I called to tell him there may be fossils buried in land that belongs to the neighborhood."

"But he was talking about millions of dollars!" said Jack.

"Yeah, he sounded dastardly!" said I. "And he told us his name was J.D., not Mr. Dean. First clue: bad guys <u>always</u> lie about their names!"

"The D <u>is</u> for Dean. His first name is Jimbo. And I was just telling him that you kids were hoping to find a valuable skeleton," she said kindly as she wiped the mud from Jack's nose. "He's a very nice man. He's going to help us figure out what to do next. But first, all 3 of you need a bath. How about a nice dip in my Jacuzzi* tub upstairs?"

"All right," I grumbled, "but I'm still not sure about that jolly* Dean giant..."

Mrs. Lopez gave us swim trunks for privacy, then Jack and Tommy and I had a long soak in the Jacuzzi, which is not weird because it's more like a hot tub than a bathtub.

We got nice and wrinkly as we filled Tommy in on the whole Jackosaurus story. Afterward Mrs. Lopez gave us Mexican hot chocolate (it's got cinnamon in it!) and put in another one of those movies-in-a-Very-Humongous-Sized-plastic-box: Indiana Jones and the Last Crusade.

I fell asleep during the movie and dreamed of saving a Triceratops skeleton made of gold from a team of bad guys wearing skirts over their suits of armor. What?! They were scary!

Looking back, we only heard J.D.'s side of the conversation. The whole thing went more like this:

TRICERATITAN

SPIKY ARMOR FROM HEAD TO TOE

POISON-TIPPED HORNS AND JAVELIN*

12 FEET TALL

STAYS STRONG EATING MEAT AND BACON

I'M OLD AND BOLD AND UNCONTROLLED.

12-PACK ABS

TAIL FOR WHIPPING AT ENEMIES (ALSO DOUBLES AS A STOOL)

SWIM TRUNKS FOR PRIVACY

JOSIE AND THE KIDS-IN-HATS

Since today was Sunday and we had a full day of kid freedom ahead of us, we convinced Mrs. Lopez to call Josie and invite her to Fort Collins. We were super excited when she said yes!

So at 2 o'clock this afternoon, Josie pulled up at Jack's house, and the whole bunch of us walked over to the Jackosaurus ditch.

"It's muddy," I warned her.

"This isn't my first dino dig," she said, pointing to her knee-high rubber boots.

We all jumped down into the ditch. Jack and I reenacted the fateful leg-rescuing episode. Josie took pictures of the ditch and of us holding the Jackosaurus fossil as we pointed to where it had come out of the ground.

Pretty soon Mr. Dean came along. In his jocular* way, he reminded us all to call him J.D.

"I understand the neighborhood owns this ditch and this field. Is that right, J.D.?" asked Josie.

"Yep. I even checked with an attorney who lives in Jackalope Junction to make sure," he said.

"So is it OK with you if I stick my hands into the mud on the ditch embankment and feel around a little bit?" she asked.

"I don't see why not!" he said. "That won't hurt anything. Whaddya think, Jovana?"

"In the name of science, I say go for it!" said Mrs. Lopez.

Without further ado, Josie rolled her sweatshirt sleeves up to her elbows and plunged her right arm into the ditch wall, at the exact spot where we'd told her the Jackosaurus fossil had come flying out.

"Do you want to help me, Jack?" she asked.

Jack practically exploded with joy as he stuck his arms into the mud alongside hers.

All that happened for a minute or 2 was slurpy silence. Then Josie said, "I think I feel a face of solid rock back in here. A vertical strata of some kind. Can you feel it, Jack?"

"Yes!" he shouted. "What type is it?"

"I don't think we can tell that without clearing some of the topsoil away. J.D. and Jovana, is it OK if we scrape off some of this mud in a little section here to see what's underneath?"

TENNIS BALLS ARE TO DOGS WHAT ROCKS ARE TO JACK.

"Heck, my dog's done more damage digging for tennis balls in this field," said J.D. "Scrape away!"

So Josie and Jack wiped away some of the mud sticking to the wall. The ground was so wet that it came off super easy, in big clumps.

Then Josie stopped and turned her head sideways to look at Jack. "Do you see what I see?" she asked.

He studied the exposed stone, then he locked eyes with Josie. "Are those stripes of purple and green shale? Oh wow."

"Sure looks like it," Josie said. She had that same rock ecstasy look in her eyes as Jack. "I feel some loose stones here. Let's clear away a little more."

After a few more minutes of mud grabbing, I couldn't take it anymore. "So is there a whole Jackosaurus in there or not?" I asked.

"Once we rinse off this section, we'll be able to see the true colors of the stratum," said Josie, "but the composition of sedimentary layering indicates that we may have found the Morrison Formation, a <u>Jurassic</u>-aged rock formation, which would be unusual in this area. If this <u>is</u> Jurassic shale, it could very well mean that..."

She was starting to lose me with all that rock jargon, when—

HOLY SMOKES HOLY SMOKES HOLY SMOKES!!!

And in Jack's muddy hands was a muddy rock that looked like it had...giant muddy <u>teeth</u> sticking out of it!

91

Everyone in the ditch crowded around Jack to see the find up closer.

"Jack, that is definitely part of a jawbone, with teeth still intact," said Josie. "And look, boys, these small bits of jagged* stone aren't just pieces of crumbling shale—some of them are fossil fragments as well! Holy smokes is right!"

Everyone was high-fiving and hugging and taking pictures with their phones when I heard a new voice from the air above me.

"Hey! Did you guys find more buried treasure?" I'll give you one guess who it was and what kind of hat she was wearing.

WELL, WELL, WELL...

"Bee!" cried Jack. "We found a jawbone-with-teeth from a Jurassic dinosaur! Come look!"

Bee jumped down into the ditch, and Jack and Josie filled her in on our fossil finds so far. The three of them talked in fast-forward, like chipmunks who'd eaten too many jellybeans.

No MATTER WHAT THEY TELL YOU, YOU CAN <u>NEVER</u> HAVE TOO MUCH SUGAR.

IT'S THE BEGINNING OF JELLYBEAN SEASON, SO WE'D BETTER STOCK UP.

Mrs. Lopez and J.D. had climbed out of the ditch by now and were also chattering happily, only in a slower, more grown-up way, like parent chipmunks who've had just a <u>couple</u> jellybeans. I scrambled out and joined them.

"So should we go get our shovels?" I asked. "We've got our expert paleontologist here, and also you guys, our neighborhood grown-ups. That's everything we need to start digging, right?"

This time it was J.D. who reached out to shake <u>my</u> hand.

Speech bubble: ALDO, YOU AND JACK SHOULD FEEL VERY PROUD.

Speech bubble: THIS IS THE MOST REMARKABLE THING TO HAPPEN IN JACKALOPE JUNCTION IN YEARS!

"Look, you guys," J.D. continued, "I'm jonesin'* to dig too. But we can't...at least not until the home owners' association—the HOA— votes on what to do about this. Mrs. Lopez and I don't have the authority to decide by ourselves."

"Geeeeez!" I groaned. "Why does there have to be so so much grown-up authorizing all the time?"

Mrs. Lopez put her arm around me in a sideways hug. "The good news," she said, "is there happens to be an HOA meeting tomorrow night! You won't have to wait much longer."

So now you know what I know. Jack took the dino teeth home to clean them (and probably lick them, ew!). He said he'd lock them in the case with the other Jackosaurus fossil. Josie's coming back tomorrow for the HOA meeting. Jack and Tommy and I are gonna go to the meeting too. So is Bee, because she lives in this neighborhood, which makes her a 1/200th owner, just like me. *Blerg.*

But before I go play my trumpet—my mom is telling me I have to even though I'm basically the next Indiana Jones, and everybody knows Indy doesn't do boring things like practice—I just have to say one final thing:

Finders keepers is justice.* Anything else is totally not fair.

CLEAN TEETH ARE HAPPY TEETH!

...AND JUSTICE FOR ALL (NOT)

You know how sports teams have captains—
the jockiest* players who are the leaders? Welp, it
turns out neighborhoods have a <u>bunch</u> of captains.
They're grown-ups who meet and talk about
all the neighborhood "problems" and what to do
about them. Here's what happens at home owners'
association meetings:

YES,
ROOFING
SHINGLES
ARE MY
FAVORITE
TOPIC.

WE SHOULD
TALK ABOUT
THAT CRACK IN
THE SIDEWALK
FOR AT LEAST
AN HOUR.

ON THE MATTER OF
POOL LANDSCAPING, THE
BOARD CAN'T DECIDE
BETWEEN A JAPANESE
LILAC OR A JUNIPER...
SHALL WE OPEN IT UP
FOR DISCUSSION?

ZZZZ.

Anyways, after an excessive amount of boringness, Josie finally showed up, and the grown-ups finally got around to talking about the one topic worth talking about: the Jackosaurus.

There was explaining about the stuck leg and the ground burp and the rock-fossil and the pawn shop and the museum visit and Josie checking out the ditch and the purple-green rock under the mud and Jack and the toothy jawbone, then Josie said,

"I've contacted my colleagues at the Museum of Nature & Science in Denver. They'd like to bring their team and equipment to the Jackalope Junction ditch and do a dig. At first they'd dig with small trowels, to find the perimeter of the bone bed, then they'd use regular shovels to expose the block of ground that contains the fossils. After protecting it with layers of plaster, they'd use heavy equipment to remove the block from the ground and load it into a big truck. Once it reaches the lab in Denver, museum experts and volunteers would separate the rock from the fossils."

IT'S CALLED A BONE BED BECAUSE BONES SLEEP THERE FOR AGES!

97

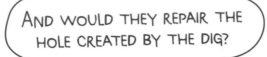

AND WOULD THEY REPAIR THE HOLE CREATED BY THE DIG?

said Mr. Jablonski, one of the neighborhood captains.

"Yes, they'd bring in fill dirt to patch the hole," said Josie.

AND HOW WILL THEY KEEP THE AREA SAFE WHILE YOU'RE DIGGING?

asked Mrs. Jocund pleasantly.

"They'll put up an 8-foot construction fence around the perimeter, with a locked gate, on the day digging begins," said Josie.

AND WHAT IF THERE'S A WHOLE JACKOSAURUS DOWN THERE THAT'S WORTH A LOT OF MONEY?

"Since the museum is paying for the dig, they would like the neighborhood to donate any fossils they might find to become part of their collection," Josie said. "But I asked them if you and Jack could name the fossil site—and the species, if it turns out to be a new one—and they've agreed."

That's when tears started sliding down Jack's skinny brown cheeks.

I glared at Josie. "See what you did?!" I accused. "You made Jack cry! We trusted you and you jeopardized* our dreams." Then I turned to Jack. "We don't need the museum people anyway! Your mom could sell Jackosaurus on eBay for us. Let's dig him up ourselves! I'm gonna go get my shovel right now..."

"It's not about the money, Aldo!" blubbed Jack. "It's just...I get to be part of a real, live dinosaur dig—and the site is going to be named after me! This is my dream coming true! I'm so happy!"

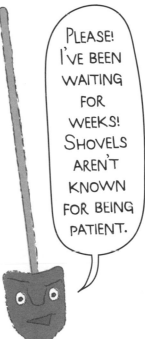

PLEASE! I'VE BEEN WAITING FOR WEEKS! SHOVELS AREN'T KNOWN FOR BEING PATIENT.

After that, I sat in stunned silence as the neighborhood captains voted to a) let the museum dig and b) donate Jackosaurus. No finders keepers. Only losers weepers. No fortune. Only a tiny bit of glory.

Is that justice? I'll let you be the judge.

THE GLORY OF GLORY

I'm back. It's been a few days since I've journaled. Jack is all happy with the way things are turning out, but <u>my</u> dream didn't come true— and that has made me sad. Too sad to write and draw. Just the right amount of sad to wrap myself in a blanket and watch TV (except not *Pawn Store*, because of the reminding).

But have you noticed that whenever you're stuck in the mud of your sadness, something you're not expecting comes along and pulls you out into the fizzy joy of aliveness? (Mr. Mot calls it *joie de vivre*.* Which to me sounds like a casserole.)

That's what happened to me today. (The joy part, not the casserole.) This morning at school, Mr. Krug called me and Jack to the front of our 5th grade classroom. I thought we were in trouble for forgetting to take off our Indy hats, but no! The Kruginator was holding a copy of our school newsletter, the *Dana Elementary Dispatch*.

"Exciting news!" he announced to the class. "We have paleontologists in our midst!" And he read this article out loud:

Students Make Dino-rific Discovery
by Bee Goode

Fifth graders Jack Lopez and Aldo Zelnick have made an important paleontological discovery. While playing in a ditch near their homes in Jackalope Junction, they found a special rock.

"After I washed it off, I realized it was a fossil," said Lopez, age 10.

The boys showed the fossil to Josie Jefferson, a paleontologist in training at the University of Colorado. Further analysis revealed that underground near the ditch lies an unusual deposit of Morrison Formation. About 150 million years old, the wall of rock is from the Jurassic period and often holds dinosaur fossils.

So far the team has found two fossils at the site—a jawbone with teeth, and what may be part of a hip bone. Experts from the Museum of Nature & Science in Denver will soon excavate the site in search of more fossils. The Jackalope Junction neighbors have voted to donate any fossils that might be found to the museum.

Zelnick could not be reached for comment.

SO <u>THAT'S</u> WHY SHE KEPT TRYING TO TALK TO ME AT RECESS...

The whole class clapped! Mr. Krug shook our hands and took a picture of us holding the newsletter. And our classmates asked me and Jack so many questions that we missed Grammar. Yesss!

Then, after school, Jack and I were walking to my house when we noticed some random 3rd graders poking around the Jackosaurus ditch!

"Hey, what do you guys think you're doing?" I shouted.

"We're lookin' for dinosaur bones!" jeered* a kid with pointy hair.

"Oh no you're not!" yelled Jack, and he ran at them with a fury rarely seen except in Lord of the Rings movies.

The rugrats scattered, but Jack and I stood guard for a while to make sure they weren't coming back.

"The site's been compromised!" said Jack, pacing back and forth. "Now that other people know where he is, Jackosaurus isn't safe."

"You're right," I realized. "Every jughead* from here to Johnstown is gonna wanna find a fossil in our fossil bed!"

"We can't let that happen," said Jack, throwing his arms into the air. "We have to protect it."

"Yeah! We'll protect it! Wait...How?"

"It's Friday afternoon. So we'll just...camp here all weekend."

"We will?" I was looking around and noticing the lack of electrical plug-ins and cushiony places to sit down. And general heat and shelter. And <u>food</u>.

"You stay here and stand guard," said Jack. "I'll go get my dad. He's good at camping."

So I sat down criss-cross applesauce on the damp, March-brown grass that grew over Jackosaurus's grave. *I wonder how he died?* I thought. *I wonder what he had for his last meal? I wonder if he always wanted to be a fossil?*

In a jiffy* Jack came back with Fritz (that's his dad), and I went to my house to tell my parents I'd be by the ditch if they needed me. I filled my backpack with flashlights, my Game Boy, junk food,* and this sketchbook. I whistled for my trusty partner, Max, and he followed me outside.

By the time I got back to the ditch, Jack and Fritz had our guard station all set up.

"I know you boys have everything under control here," said Fritz. "But you've got me in the mood for a camp-out myself. Would it be OK if I stayed overnight with you?"

"I guess so," I said, secretly relieved that a grown-up with firefighter muscles would be there to back us up. You know, in case of professional fortune stealers, like in the Indy movies.

Pretty soon my mom and dad brought us hot, homemade pizza and set up a folding table for us to eat from. After it got dark and we

LIKE I ALWAYS SAY, YOU KNOW YOU'RE ROUGHIN' IT WHEN THE PIZZA ONLY HAS 2 KINDS OF MEAT.

were cozy in our sleeping bags, Jack read to us from the Encyclopedia of Dinosaurs until Fritz, and then Jack, fell asleep.

Me, I'm still awake, trying to get caught up in my sketchbook. It's sorta weird camping out in the field across from my house. But it's also kinda cool. Just the right amount of adventure mixed together with my own refrigerator 200 feet away.

COLORADO JACK

It's a good thing we decided to guard Jackosaurus, because this weekend has been a nonstop parade of people coming to Jackalope Junction to see the fossil ditch. Apparently Bee's school newsletter story got the attention of the local newspaper, which ran its own story about Jackosaurus in this morning's paper. (They even interviewed me and Jack and took a picture of us holding the fossils!)

So now everyone in town knows.

And they keep turning up and getting out of
their cars and walking over to our tent, and Jack
and I keep showing the Jackosaurus fossils and
telling what happened and making sure no one does
any digging. Tommy and Bee have been here helping.
So have my parents and Jack's parents and J.D.
and Mr. Mot and my grandma, Goosy. Man, being
responsible for a dead dinosaur takes a village.

Oh boy. Here comes a white van with a
Channel 4 TV logo on its side. Gotta go.

Jack and I just got interviewed by that yellow-haired lady television reporter. We were just on the Denver news! J.D. took a short guard shift by himself so the rest of us could run over to my house and see us on TV.

SOURCES SAY THAT YOUR NEIGHBORHOOD IS DONATING THE FOSSILS TO THE MUSEUM. IS THAT CORRECT?

OF COURSE!

UNFORTUNATELY!

YOU KNOW WHAT ELSE IS UNFORTUNATE? GETTING COMBED BY MY MOM AGAIN.

After our TV debut came a giant potluck picnic. Our families and a bunch of neighbors carried food and tables and chairs to the campsite, and together we celebrated St. Patrick's Day: Dinosaur Edition. My hand is kinda sore from getting shaken so many times.

Finally it's quiet here at Camp Jackosaurus. Even though it's Sunday night, our parents are letting Jack and me camp out again. As we watched the full moon rise, we sat in our camp chairs and talked about what to name the fossil site.

The second Jack said "the Indiana Jones Fossil Site," my brain recognized its awesomeness. The name captured the adventurous, outdoorsy, dude-ish spirit of our quest for fortune and glory, even if Indiana Jones was an archaeologist, not a paleontologist, and even if it didn't include the words "Aldo" or "Jack." But wouldn't people think it was in the state of Indiana?

"How about 'The Colorado Jones Fossil Site'?" I said. "Or...I've got it! 'The Colorado Jack Fossil Site'!"

Jack didn't answer. It was dark out, but the moonlight glinted off the watery puddles covering his eyeballs. That's how I knew it was the perfect name. And how I finally felt, deep down in my own alive bones, that even though fortune (I imagine) and glory (I know) are pretty great, best friends are, for some dumb reason, greater.

The museum's dig starts tomorrow, while we're at school. Jack and I and the gang are gonna come straight here after school. I can't wait to see what they find!

THE DIG

DAY ONE – REMOVING THE "OVERBURDEN"

While Jack and I were at school today, Josie and the main paleontologist guy, Dr. Jubilee, plus some other helpers, used shovels and picks to scrape off the grass and topsoil till they got down to hard rock.

I CLIMBED A TREE SO I COULD SHOW YOU WHAT THE DIG LOOKS LIKE FROM ABOVE. THE HOLE IS ABOUT 1 JACK + 1 ALDO LONG BY 1 LONG-JACK WIDE AND 3 FEET DEEP!

LOOK! ACTUAL FOSSIL PIECES STICKING OUT OF THE ROCK!!!

CAUTION
CAUTION

Day Two - Consolidation

After school the gang and I ran straight to the fossil site, and guess what? The team had spent all day covering the exposed fossils with a bunch of toilet paper! Paleontology is weirder than I thought.

DINOSAURS GO THROUGH A <u>LOT</u> OF TOILET PAPER.

TRUST ME, I'M A GEOLOGIST

Day Four – Jacketing*

Today they wrapped the fossil block in white plaster! It looks like some kind of giant art project, but Dr. Jubilee said it's to protect Jackosaurus on the jostling* ride down to Denver. Jack also gave Josie the 2 fossil bones he'd been keeping in his case, so they'd have all the puzzle pieces.

Day Five - The Journey

We got home from school today just in time to see Jackosaurus, in his white jacket, being loaded into the back of a truck for his ride to Denver. Jack and I waved him goodbye as he rode off into the afternoon sun.

"For some reason I'm hungry for a burrito," I said. "Do you have any at your house?"

But Jack just shook his head sadly and didn't say a word.

JOHNSON'S CORNER: STOP FOR CINNAMON ROLLS

THE GREAT ROCKY MOUNTAINS

↑ MINI EXCAVATOR! THAT'S GOING ON MY CHRISTMAS LIST THIS YEAR FOR SURE...

DENVER

ADIÓS, AMIGO

It's the day after Jackosaurus got trucked away. Jack and my mom and Goosy and I walked over to the Colorado Jack Fossil Site. Workers were busy filling the hole with dirt then covering up the dirt with strips of grass. But, I noticed, that didn't fill the dinosaur-sized hole in our hearts where Jackosaurus lived for the past 3 weeks. I guess that's why Jack seemed so glum yesterday.

"Don't forget!" I said, trying to cheer him up. "Dr. Jubilee invited us to visit Jackosaurus at the museum in Denver in about a week, after they've had a chance to get the rest of the fossil bones out of the rock block."

"The grown-ups have been talking," said Mom, "and we have an idea. Since you boys have spring break next week, and since you're dinosaur explorers now, how about we all go on a junket* to Dinosaur National Monument for the weekend?"

"What's that?" I asked.

"Only the most important fossil site in Colorado...and practically the world!" cried Jack, perking up a jillion percent. "It's on my bucket list!"

"It's a 6-hour road-trip from here," said Goosy. "And what's a road-trip without copious candy? Would anyone like to accompany me to the candy store this afternoon? My treat?"

"Uh, me!" I said. "My bucket list is half candy stores!"

So Goosy and Jack and I are going candy shopping after lunch. Turns out dino finders get some just deserts* after all!

ALDO'S BUCKET LIST DU JOUR*

10. Jakarta, Indonesia, for gado-gado (stir fry with peanut sauce—yumbo!)

9. Fuzziwig's Candy Factory Steamboat Springs, Colorado

8. Japan, to meet ninjas and visit Papabubble in Tokyo

7. Jupiter (the planet)

6. Sweet! candy store Hollywood, California

5. New York City (for pizza!)

4. The Jell-O Museum Le Roy, New York

3. The Sweet Palace Philipsburg, Montana

2. Candylicious Dubai

1. Jackson Hole, Wyoming, for skiing (not!)

JUJUBES*

This afternoon I was like a kid in a candy store.

That's because Goosy, best grandma ever, took me and Jack to Jujubes to stockpile us with sugary deliciousness for our road trip to Dinosaur National Monument!

Jujubes is a candy shop like Toys R Us is a toy shop. I'm talking floor-to-ceiling, wall-to-wall shelves and bins and jars jam-packed with every sweet you've ever heard of and lots you haven't.

They had chocolate galore. They had all the
rares, like Bottle Caps and Zotz. They had weird
grandma stuff that Goosy kept exclaiming about,
like Necco Wafers and Charleston Chews. They
also had gummy bacon, fish-head lollipops, and
unicorn boogers (kinda like Nerds but in rainbow
colors in a clear plastic tube) and so much more.

I wanted it all.

"Can I have it all?" I asked Goosy.

"I'll give you each $5 to spend," Goosy said.

Not that she wasn't generous, but that narrowed things down quite a bit.

Jack went with his old standbys: rock candy, a pack of Pop Rocks, and, in honor of our spring-break destination, a few gummy dinosaurs from one of those bins where you scoop as much as you can afford into a plastic sack.

But I could not decide! My feet and brain even started to hurt from all the walking around and considering. Goosy and Jack had already checked out, and Goosy was starting to look at her watch! So right there in Jujubes, I plopped down onto the floor and criss-cross applesauced into a yoga pose, just like Mr. Mot taught me last summer. I closed my eyes and concentrated on my breathing. (Weird, I know, but it's supposed to reset your mind.)

After 5 slow breaths in and out, I opened my eyes and *bam!* There, right in front of me, at yoga eye level, sat a jawbreaker bigger than a baseball.

"This is it!" I yelled. "I found the perfect road-trip candy!"

I sprinted to the cash register and the Jujubes guy rang up my selection.

"$9.87," he said.

"Say what?" I said.

"9 dollars and 87 cents," he repeated. "Including tax."

I turned to Goosy, raised my eyebrows, and gave her an oversized grin. "He-he...," I said to her. "I could give you $5 from my future allowances, after I pay back Timothy for the unfortunate demolished headphones incident that occurred last week?"

I'M JUDICIOUS* WITH MY FUNDS! WHAT CAN I SAY?

"Not to worry," she said as she handed the guy a $10 bill. "I'll take it out in trade."

Turns out that "trade" means taking down and boxing up a bunch of Christmas lights in her yard that she hadn't gotten around to yet.

Oh well. It was worth it. This jawbreaker is gonna be a sweet accessory for our prehistorically awesome spring break weekend.

DINOSAUR NATIONAL MONUMENT: THE WAY THERE

We're packed into the minivan on our way to Dinosaur National Monument—me, my family, Jack, and Mrs. Lopez. I've been licking my jawbreaker and reading that *Journey to the Center of the Earth* book Mr. Mot gave me. It's an old-timey story about this college kid and his crazy uncle who go to Iceland to climb inside an extinct volcano. It turns out that deep-down underneath the volcano are a bunch of rock tunnels they get lost in and ancient seas and dinosaurish creatures that try to eat them, etc.

The farther the explorers tunneled into the earth, the flatter my jawbreaker got on one side.

"I'm thinking of a dinosaur!" Jack just called out. "Go!"

Ope. Gotta put away my sketchbook so we can play 20 Questions!

THE EARTH IS MADE OF LAYERS, JUST LIKE THIS JAWBREAKER. WEIRD.

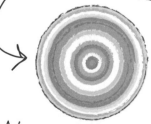

WE FOUND JACKOSAURUS IN A SPECIAL JURASSIC LAYER. EW...THAT REMINDS ME OF WHEN JACK LICKED JACKOSAURUS...

DINOSAUR NATIONAL MONUMENT: THE WAY BACK

> STEGOSAURUS IS MY NAME, SPIKY TAIL ATTACK IS MY GAME.

So it turns out that Dinosaur National Monument isn't a theme park full of giant dinosaur skeletons and statues, which is what I <u>thought</u> it was gonna be. It's actually a ginormous (like 300 square miles!) rocky wilderness, with craggy mountains, dirt roads, green rivers, and poky sagebrush.

Think Disney World but without the rides or cartoon characters or places to eat or colors besides brown (mostly) and green (a tiny bit). *Blerg.*

HERE'S A BIRD'S-EYE VIEW:

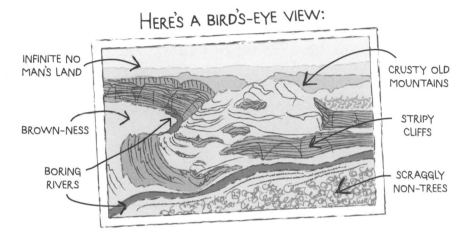

INFINITE NO MAN'S LAND

CRUSTY OLD MOUNTAINS

BROWN-NESS

STRIPY CLIFFS

BORING RIVERS

SCRAGGLY NON-TREES

The day we got there, we didn't go into the park cuz there wasn't time. Instead we checked into the Dinosaur Inn (which did have a big green dinosaur statue in the parking lot), then we went out to dinner and afterwards, played Jenga in our hotel room. (My brother, Timothy, won, of course.)

It was the <u>next</u> morning that we finally drove into the park and got to see some dinosaur bones, at the Dinosaur Quarry Exhibit Hall.

GET YOUR DINOS HERE!

Inside the Quarry building is a massive, slanty wall of rock with dinosaur fossils sticking out all over it—more than 1,600 bones from a bunch of different kinds of dinosaurs, the park ranger told us.

Everyone laughed when I said, "All the genuses are mixed together, like dinosaur soup!"

Besides the Quarry, which was pretty awesome, we did some not-as-awesome hiking on the Fossil Discovery Trail. Basically you walk for miles on a dirt path, and all around you are boring rock walls and boulders. But if you look super carefully, here and there you can spot fossils hiding in the rocks. It's like an I Spy Extinct Animals game. Which Jack wanted to play for <u>hours</u>.

LOOK! ANOTHER CLAM FOSSIL! THAT'S BECAUSE THIS WHOLE AREA USED TO BE UNDERWATER!

YUP. THAT WAS THE ONE THAT PUSHED ME OVER THE EDGE. I'M NOW OFFICIALLY FOSSILED OUT.

That night we stayed at the hotel again, and the next day we drove to the Utah Field House of Natural History (somewheres we must've crossed from Colorado into Utah). Now, that place <u>does</u> have a jillion dinosaur skeletons and statues, including some good ones like T. rex and some boringish ones like Stegosaurus, plus extinct mammals like wooly mammoths and saber-toothed tigers.

(Wow. I just looked back at the chart that Josie made for us, on page 72. Jurassic dinosaurs like Jackosaurus are about 150 million years <u>older</u> than mammoths and saber-tooths. No wonder they're not in movies together.)

After the Field House we had lunch, then Mom made me and Jack and Timothy pose by the freaky T. rex statue at the edge of town. Say "dinosaur!" she giggled as she took our picture.

EASTER'S JUST A FEW WEEKS AWAY, SO SOMEBODY THOUGHT IT WAS A GOOD IDEA TO DRESS UP POOR T. REX IN BUNNY EARS AND AN EASTER BASKET.

Now we're in the van on the drive home. Jack's got his face buried in the dinosaur encyclopedia again, and I need to finish *Journey to the Center of the Earth* for my book report that's due next week, after spring break's over.

I hope Dr. Jubilee calls me and Jack soon. I have a feeling that Jackosaurus misses us. Plus, I can't wait to see what kind of dinosaur he turns out to be...

STEGOBOT

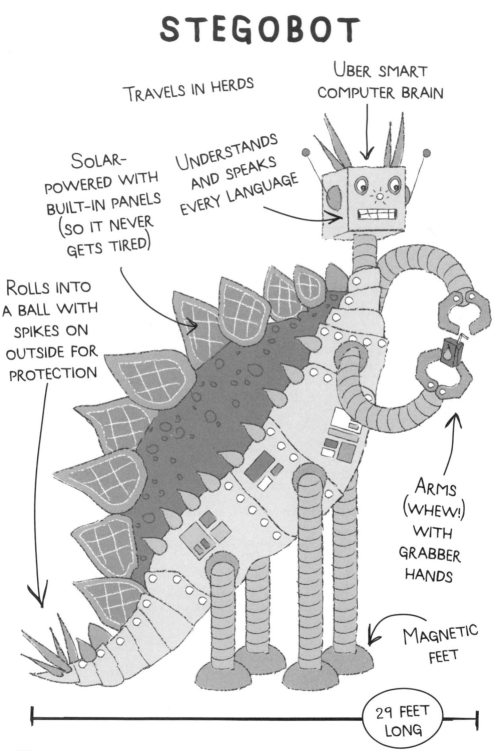

TRAVELS IN HERDS

UBER SMART COMPUTER BRAIN

SOLAR-POWERED WITH BUILT-IN PANELS (SO IT NEVER GETS TIRED)

UNDERSTANDS AND SPEAKS EVERY LANGUAGE

ROLLS INTO A BALL WITH SPIKES ON OUTSIDE FOR PROTECTION

ARMS (WHEW!) WITH GRABBER HANDS

MAGNETIC FEET

29 FEET LONG

THE CALL!

It's been a few spring-break days since we got home from our trip to Dinosaur National Monument. Jack and Tommy and Bee and I have been hanging out, playing video games and Jurassic Park (the board game), and generally basking in school-lessness.

Whenever my mom kicks us outside for some FRESH AIR, Bee's been making us jump rope with her in the driveway. Let's just say that flying rope and I still don't get along.

Then finally, this morning, Mrs. Lopez got the call from Dr. Jubilee! We're invited to the Denver museum tomorrow to see all of Jackosaurus in the flesh! Well, not in the flesh...more like in the bone... but, you know what I mean. They've chiseled his bones out of the rock block, and they've put him back together, like a prehistoric Lego set.

Tomorrow Mrs. Lopez is taking all of us to the museum! Ah geez, here I go again, getting all excited about fossils and <u>more</u> museum visits. Seriously. After tomorrow I'm gonna jettison* this Indiana Jones hat.

IT'S TIME I LET ANOTHER BOLD ADVENTURER TAKE A TURN. THE HAT'S ALL YOURS, BOGUS.

I GUESS THIS IS AS CLOSE TO FORTUNE AND GLORY AS I'M GONNA GET. WOO-HOO.

WE BE JAMMIN'

TWO-FER

Welp, today we drove to Denver and strode into the Museum of Nature & Science. It's huge! The biggest museum we've been to. And it's got <u>loads</u> of dinosaur skeletons.

We went straight to the Prehistoric Journey room, since that's where the dino action is. I can't even describe the skeletons they have, cuz to tell you the truth, all the dinosaurs we've been talking about and looking at in books and seeing in parks and museums are starting to jumble* together in my brain. Like dinosaur soup.

After we looked at the exhibits for a while, Dr. Jubilee and Josie came to get us. They took us back to their Earth Sciences Lab, which is a special behind-the-scenes area where the museum experts and volunteers separate fossils from rock and get them ready for display.

We walked by shelf after shelf of fossils, and grown-ups in white lab coats looking through microscopes and picking at fossil bones with tiny metal scrapers. We stopped at a table where 2 ladies were chiseling the plaster jacket off a dinosaur burrito from a different fossil site.

Dr. Jubilee was explaining
all the steps our Jackosaurus
burrito went through after
it got to the museum,
but I wasn't paying much
attention. I just wanted to see
Jackosaurus! So I backed slowly
and casually away from our group,
all the while looking around
for a put-together dinosaur.

Finally I'd backed up far
enough that I could see into
another room, around the
corner, and there stood
two dinosaurs. A notecard
was taped to the room's door,
and printed neatly on it were
two words: Colorado Jack.

"Wow!" I cried. "Look!"

Jack, Tommy, and Bee
came running, and we crowded around
the skeletons.

"There are 2 of them!" said Jack.

"I thought they'd be gigantic," said Tommy, sounding unusually jaded*.

"They're juveniles,*" smiled Josie. "Probably adolescents."

"What kind are they?" asked Bee.

Dr. Jubilee pointed to the one that looked like a mini-T. rex. "This is the fellow whose teeth and hip-bone you found, Jack. He's a Torvosaurus."

THE PIECES WE FOUND WENT HERE AND HERE.

Jack gasped. "That's a megalosaurid theropod!"

"You're right!" said Josie. "He was a fierce meat-eater. In fact his name means 'savage lizard.'"

"What about the other one?" asked Bee.

Even I could tell what the other skeleton was. "That's obviously a Stegosaurus," I said.

"Right again!" said Josie. "Stegosaurus is Colorado's official state fossil. He was a thyreophoran."

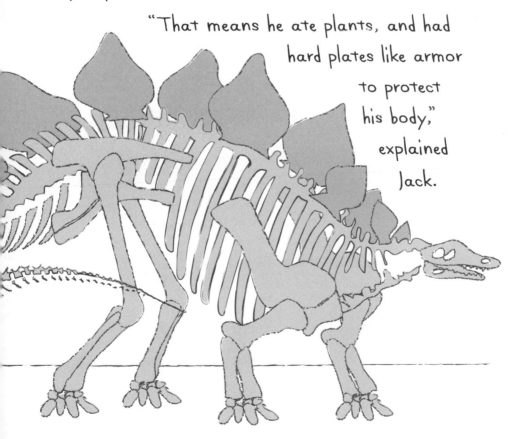

"That means he ate plants, and had hard plates like armor to protect his body," explained Jack.

"Are they boys?" asked Bee, who was taking notes on her journalist's notepad.

"We can't tell," said Josie.

"Complete dinosaur skeletons are extremely rare," said Dr. Jubilee. "And complete juvenile skeletons are even more rare. To find 2 together, of different genera nonetheless, in one bone bed... well, you boys have made a truly significant contribution to paleontology."

It was at this moment that I felt my heart grow 3 sizes. Maybe I was having another brain attack, but suddenly "making a contribution" felt even joyfuller than my fortune-and-glory dreams had.

I could also feel the dangerous lump in my throat and burning behind my eyeballs that signal I'm about to spring a leak. So I accidentally-on-purpose reached over and flicked Bee's journalist hat off her head. You know, to pull myself together.

Mrs. Lopez took lots of pictures of Jack
and me standing next to our dinosaurs, and also
a bunch that included Bee, Tommy, Josie, and Dr.
Jubilee, who said the skeletons would soon be placed
in the Prehistoric Journey room and that he was
giving us museum passes, so we could come visit
them whenever we wanted.

A while later, as we were getting ready to
leave, something occurred to me. "Wait a sec," I
said. "Wouldn't Torvosaurus and Stegosaurus be
enemies? How did they end up together like that?"

"We don't know," said Josie. "What do you
kids think?"

"I think...," said Jack slowly. "I think they
lived in the same neighborhood and they grew up
together, so...even though they weren't that much
alike...they were...friends."

"Pffft. I think the Torvosaurus was about
to eat the Stegosaurus when they both got
stuck in the mud," I said. But secretly I liked Jack's
explanation better.

On the ride home, we decided that we'd still think of the Torvosaurus as "Jackosaurus." And Jack said we should name the Stegosaurus "Aldosaurus."

"Why do I have to be the short, fat one?" I asked as I licked on my linty jawbreaker.

"Cuz the plates along his back look kinda like your hair," said Jack.

What can I say? When Jack's right, he's right.

SOME THINGS NEVER CHANGE.

DINOSAUR NATIONAL FORT

Today was the last day of spring break. It was a warm, windy Sunday, and Jack and Tommy and Bee and I met at our real, outside fort under the giant pine tree...just a Torvo-length away from the filled-in Colorado Jack Fossil Site.

We sat quietly for a while and munched on the dinosaur poop cookies my dad and I made this morning.

No-Bake Dinosaur Poop Cookies

- 1 STICK BUTTER
- 5 TABLESPOONS COCOA POWDER
- 2 CUPS SUGAR
- ¼-CUP MILK
- ¼-CUP CREAM
- ¼-TEASPOON SALT
- 1 TEASPOON VANILLA
- 4 CUPS QUICK ROLLED OATS

NOT BAD! NOT BAD AT ALL!

IGUANODON GIVES THESE COOKIES 2 THUMBS UP!

PUT BUTTER, COCOA, SUGAR AND MILK IN A BOWL. HEAT IN MICROWAVE UNTIL BUTTER IS MELTED. WHISK INGREDIENTS TOGETHER. ADD EVERYTHING ELSE. STIR WELL AND DROP BY SPOONFULS ONTO WAX PAPER. LET COOL AND HARDEN. ENJOY WITH LEMONADE. (JK!)

"Fossilized dinosaur dung is actually a thing." mused Jack. "It's called 'coprolite.' Paleontologists study it to find out what dinosaurs ate."

"Awesome!" said Tommy.

"Ew!" I said. "Wait, how big is a T. rex turd?"

"One of the biggest ever found was 25 inches long and 7 inches wide," said Jack.

"Whoa...," I said. "That's about the same size as Slate!"

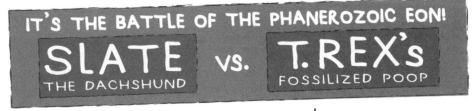

IT'S THE BATTLE OF THE PHANEROZOIC EON!
SLATE vs. T.REX's
THE DACHSHUND   FOSSILIZED POOP

IN THIS CORNER,
WEIGHING IN AT 20 POUNDS:
THE STINK

IN THIS CORNER,
WEIGHING IN AT 16 POUNDS:
THE STANK

"I think we should make a sign," said Bee.

"About dinosaur dooky?" I asked. "Cuz that's dumb. Actually, that's kinda cool..."

"No!" said Bee. "A sign to mark the Colorado Jack Fossil Site. It would let everyone know what was found there. And who found it. And when."

Jack smiled. "My dad would help us make a sign," he said.

"Let's do it!" said Tommy.

So that's how we wrapped up our spring break—and our Jurassic adventure.

WHILE WE WERE AT IT,
WE MADE 2 SIGNS.

COLORADO JACK
& FOSSIL SITE

DINOSAUR
NATIONAL
FORT

"J" GALLERY

Mr. Mot used to be an English teacher. He's a word nerd, and he likes to help me use awesome words in my sketchbooks. I mark the best words with one of these:* (it's called an asterisk). When you see an * you'll know you can look here, in the Gallery, to see what the word means. If you don't know how to say some of the words, just ask Mr. Mot. Or someone you know who's like Mr. Mot. Or go to aldozelnick.com, and we'll say them for you.

Ⓗ This symbol means that the J is pronounced like an H.

jabbering (pg. 19): talking and talking and talking away, sometimes when no one's even listening

jacketing (pg. 114): wrapping a chunk of rock that contains fossils in a plaster cast. The plaster goes on wet but dries hard, like a piñata.

I LOVE MY JOB.

jackhammers (pg. 113): a kind of power tool that smashes a chisel up and down repeatedly in order to demolish something. Awesome!

jackpot (pg. 23): a bunch of money you more or less win (as opposed to working for it). That pot of gold at the end of the rainbow? It's a jackpot.

jackrabbit (pg. 52): So, a jackrabbit is actually a kind of hare, not a rabbit. Who's in charge of these things? Sheesh.

jack squat (pg. 66): nothing, *nada*, zero, zip, zilch, bupkis

Jacuzzi (pg. 83): a kind of bathtub with water jets that move the water around and make it bubbly and massage-y

jaded (pg. 136): expecting something to be bad or boring because you've noticed that it's bad or boring in the past

jagged (pg. 92): uneven and pointy around the outside

jaguar (pg. 20): a kind of wild, big cat (think tiger but with spots instead of stripes and a little smaller) that lives in Mexico and South America. Even the solid black ones have spots.

THIS STUFF IS MUY CALIENTE!

Ⓗ **jalapeño** (pg. 27): a spicy green chile pepper (I stuck a piece on the cover.)

jambalaya (pg. 13): a spicy stew made with sausage and shrimp and chicken (3 meats!) and some vegetables and rice (but you can pick out the veggies)

jammies (pg. 57): cozy pajamas

Ⓗ **jamon-y-huevos** (pg. 62): ham-and-eggs, baby!

jam-packed (pg. 28): stuffed totally full

jargon (pg. 28): special words you use for a certain topic or specialty

Jay-Z (pg. 13): a rapper Timothy likes

jazzed (pg. 57): excited

je ne sais quois (pg. 160): "I don't know what," it says in French. But really...it means "a certain special something."

YOU'RE JUST JEALOUS OF MY SWEET HAT.

NOT SO MUCH. IF YOU HAD A JAVELIN, THOUGH, I'D TAKE THAT.

jauntier (pg. 34): more cheerful and lively

javelin (pg. 86): a really long, pointy spear used as a weapon in ancient times but now thrown just to see how far it can be thrown. Uh, yeah...

jealous (pg. 43): wishing you could be as awesome or loved as someone else. For more coolness, say "jelly" instead.

jeepers (pg. 18): an expression that means "holy cow!" or "wow!"

jeered (pg. 102): said loudly and disrespectfully in an "I can do whatever I want" way

Jekyll and Hyde (pg. 81): this famous character from some old book who was half nice, half mean

jelly-bellied (pg. 52): chubby, especially in the gut area

jeopardized (pg. 99): put in danger of being ruined or taken away

jets, cool your (pg. 29): Calm down!

jettison (pg. 132): get rid of because you don't need it anymore

jeweler's glasses (pg. 26): They're basically microscopes and glasses and lights made into one cool gadget.

jewelry (pg. 13): Um, hello? You know what jewelry is. Do I have to tell you everything?

jibes (pg. 71): goes along well with; matches

WHICH SOCKS JIBE?

Ⓗ **jicama** (pg. 51): a crunchy, white vegetable that tastes halfway between an apple and a water chestnut and an Asian pear. In other words, pretty good—for a veggie.

jiffy (pg. 104): really fast and no-sweat-y

jiggle (pg. 23): move back and forth a little bit

147

jillions (pg. 73): a really big amount, like millions or billions, except it's a made-up number

jinxed (pg. 70): ruined by causing bad luck to happen

jittery (pg. 13): shaky and vibrate-y and weird

JK (pg. 24): Just Kidding!

Jobs, Steve (pg. 53): the guy who invented the Apple computer, iPod, iPhone, iEverything

jockiest (pg. 96): A jock is a person who's really good at sports, so the jockiest person is the best of the jocks. Timothy is the jockiest person I know.

jocular (pg. 88): happy and joking around

jogged (pg. 52): Jogging is to running as nibbling is to devouring.

joie de vivre (pg. 100): a Frenchy phrase that means "the joy of life"

jolly (pg. 83): happiness that shows on the outside

Jones, Indiana (pg. 24): a treasure-hunting, hat-wearing, adventure-having archaeologist character from the movies

jonesing (pg. 94): in the mood for; have a craving for

joshin' (pg. 85): kidding

jostling (pg. 114): moving around in a bumpy, shovy way

jouncing (pg. 22): a rough, bouncy motion

SOUP DU JOUR

jour, du (pg. 117): means "of the day" in French

WHAT'S YOUR FAVORITE SOUP DU JOUR? MINE'S FRENCH ONION, CUZ OF THE MELTED CHEESE PART.

journal (pg. 7): to write about what you do each day in a blank book. I write and draw, which means I'm twice as talented.

journalism (pg. 45): writing about the news in an honest and fair way; not to be confused with journaling, which is writing about your personal news however you feel like

jovial (pg. 81): cheerful and happy, but not in as jokey a way as jocular

joyously (pg. 25): with much happiness and spritual gratefulness

jubilant (pg. 67): super deliriously happy

judicious (pg. 122): very careful

juggernaut (pg. 41): a really strong and overpowering force

jughead (pg. 103): knucklehead; nincompoop

Ⓗ *jugo de naranja* (pg. 62): orange juice

KEEP CALM AND ASK A LOT OF QUESTIONS!

149

Juicy Fruit (pg. 26): a really sweet kind of gum that comes in a yellow package

jujitsu (pg. 80): a kind of martial art, like karate, kung fu and tae kwon do

juju (pg. 65): supernatural magic or luck

jujubes (pg. 118): a chewy fruit-flavored candy; also the name of a candy store in my town!

julienned (pg. 51): a cooking word that means cut up into skinny sticks

jumble (pg. 133): get mixed up into a mixed-up mixture

jumbo (pg. 46): the very biggest. (Hint: When ordering junk food that comes in different sizes, always ask for jumbo.)

jumping beans (pg. 13): Mexican seeds with moth babies living inside them. Weird.

jumping jacks (pg. 38): a very active movement that in real life involves arms and legs and coordination and running out of breath

jumpstarted (pg. 21): got going real quick

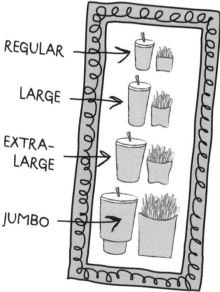

REGULAR

LARGE

EXTRA-LARGE

JUMBO

junket (pg. 116): a trip with a group of people

junk food (pg. 104): food that's more about tasting amazing than being good for you. Your body really, really wants it but doesn't "need" it, supposedly.

Jurassic (pg. 51): the middle part of the Age of Reptiles (see Josie's chart on pg. 72)

just deserts (pg. 117): what you deserve (or at least dessert!)

justice (pg. 95): what's fair and right and proper

juveniles (pg. 136): not a little kid but not a grown-up either

juxtapose (pg. 78): when you put two things beside each other (in real life OR in your mind) to compare them

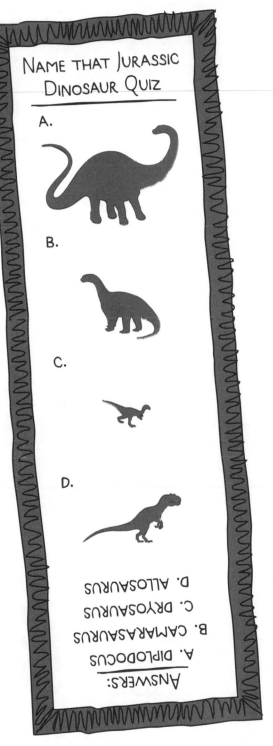

NAME THAT JURASSIC DINOSAUR QUIZ

A.

B.

C.

D.

ANSWERS:
A. DIPLODOCUS
B. CAMARASAURUS
C. DRYOSAURUS
D. ALLOSAURUS

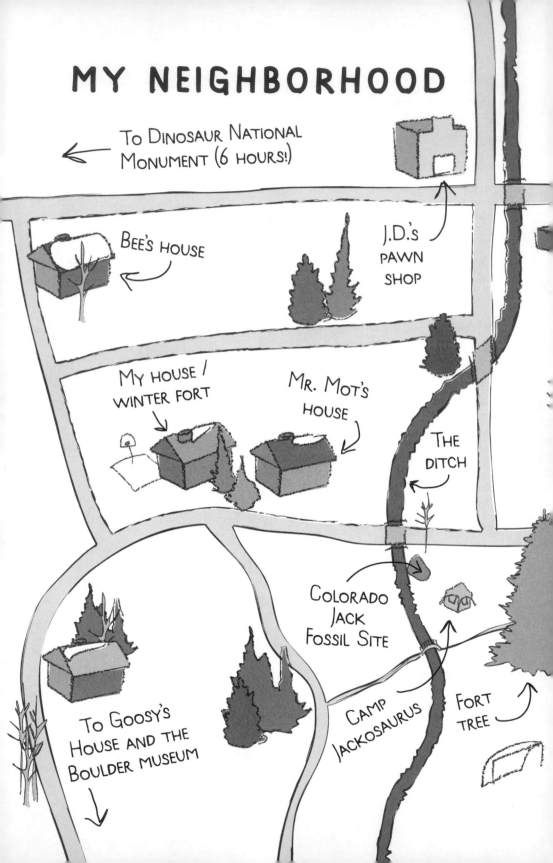

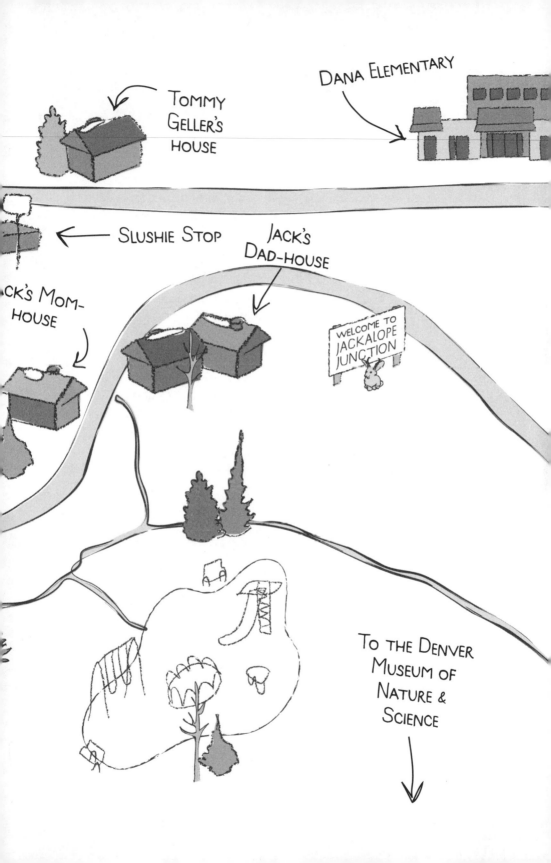

ABOUT THE award-winning ALDO ZELNICK COMIC NOVEL SERIES

The Aldo Zelnick comic novels are an alphabetical series for middle-grade readers aged 7-13. Rabid and reluctant readers alike enjoy the intelligent humor and drawings as well as the action-packed stories. They've been called vitamin-fortified *Wimpy Kids*.

NOW AVAILABLE!

160 pages | Hardcover
ISBN: 978-1-934649-04-6
$12.95

Part comic romps, part mysteries, and part sesquipedalian-fests (ask Mr. Mot), they're beloved by parents, teachers, and librarians as much as kids.

Artsy-Fartsy introduces ten-year-old Aldo, the star and narrator of the entire series, who lives with his family in Colorado. He's not athletic like his older brother, he's not a rock hound like his best friend, but he does like bacon. And when his artist grandmother, Goosy, gives him a sketchbook to "record all his artsy-fartsy ideas" during summer vacation, it turns out Aldo is a pretty good cartoonist.

In addition to an engaging cartoon story, each book in the series includes an illustrated glossary of fun and challenging words used throughout the book, such as *absurd, abominable*, and *audacious* in *Artsy-Fartsy* and *brazen*, *behemoth*, and *boisterous* in *Bogus*.

BAILIWICK PRESS

www.bailiwickpress.com | www.aldozelnick.com

ALSO IN THE ALDO ZELNICK COMIC NOVEL SERIES

ACKNOWLEDGMENTS

"Dinosaurs may be extinct from the face of the planet,
but they are alive and well in our imaginations."

— Steve Miller

Stir Aldo Zelnick and friends, Indiana Jones, and a freshly discovered fossil into your story soup and what do you get? *Jackpot!*

When Kendra was a kid, she loved dinosaurs, and she still remembers how exciting it was to visit Dinosaur National Monument when she was 10. Her generation's passion for prehistoric creatures burns bright in today's children, as well. We hope this Aldo story helps satisfy their craving for all things Cretaceous (well, Mesozoic in general).

The ethics and rigors of paleontology proved a bit challenging to jibe with Aldo's immediate instinct upon finding a fossil, which is to dig up the skeleton and see if he might be able to sell it for big bucks. Finders keepers, right? But as always with our stories, we try hard to walk the line between educational accuracy and realistic kid fun. And so we turned to paleontology professor Dr. Karen Chin and grad student Allison Vitkus at the University of Colorado Boulder's Museum of Natural History, whose suggestions helped us shape the plot and fine tune the nitty-gritty. We're so grateful for their help. Jumbo thanks, too, to Kendra's favorite real-life, hat-wearing rock hounds, sister-geologist Dana Spanjer and Dr. Joe Elkins, professor of earth science education at the University of Northern Colorado, whose guidance kept our story's stratigraphy as grounded as possible.

Of course, we must also acknowledge the regulars: jack-of-all-trades Renée; the judicious Slow Sanders; un-jaded interns Astrid and Martha; and jewel-of-a-designer Launie. To all of you, and to our families and Aldo's jovial Angels, we extend thanks of Jurassic proportion.

ALDO'S JOVIAL ANGELS

Halo There! If you're an Aldo Zelnick fan, e-mail info@bailiwickpress.com and ask for details about becoming an Aldo's Angel. Angels receive special opportunities such as pre-publication discounts, free shipping, naming rights, and listing in the acknowledgments (especially fun for kids).

Barbara Anderson

Carol & Wes Baker

Butch & Sue Byram

Michael & Pam Dobrowski

Leigh Waller Fitschen

Chris Goold

Roy Griffin

Bennett, Calvin, Beckett & Camden Halvorson

Oliver Harrison (Matthew & Erin)

Terry & Theresa Harrison

Richard & Peggy Hohm

Vicki & Bill Krug

Annette & Tom Lynch

Lisa & Kyle Miller

The Motz & Scripps Families (McCale, Alaina, Everett, Caden, Ambria & Noah)

Jackie O'Hara & Erin Rogers

Betty Oceanak

Jackie Peterson and Emma, Dorie & Elissa

John Schiller & Suzanne Holm

Slow Sand Writers Society

Barb & Steve Spanjer

Dana Spanjer

Vince & Adrianne Tranchitella

THE ALDO ZELNICK FAN CLUB
IS FOR READERS OF ANY AGE WHO
LOVE THE BOOK SERIES AND
WANT THE INSIDE SCOOP ON
ALL THINGS ZELNICKIAN.

GO TO WWW.ALDOZELNICK.COM
AND CLICK ON THIS FLAG-THINGY!

SIGN UP TO RECEIVE:

- sneak preview chapters from the next book.
- an early look at coming book titles, covers, and more.
- opportunities to vote on new character names and other stuff.
- discounts on the books and merchandise.
- a card from Aldo on your birthday (for kids)!

The Aldo Zelnick fan club is free and easy.
If you're under 13, ask your mom or dad to sign you up!

ABOUT THE AUTHOR

Karla Oceanak has been a voracious reader her whole life and a writer and editor for more than twenty years. She has also ghostwritten numerous self-help books. Karla loves doing school visits and speaking to groups about children's literacy. She lives with her husband, Scott, their three boys, and a cat named Puck in a house strewn with Legos, ping-pong balls, Pokémon cards, video games, books, and dirty socks in Fort Collins, Colorado. This is her tenth novel.

ABOUT THE ILLUSTRATOR

Kendra Spanjer divides her time between being "a writer who illustrates" and "an illustrator who writes." She decided to cultivate her artistic side after discovering that the best part of chemistry class was entertaining her peers (and her professor) with "The Daily Chem Book" comic. Since then, her diverse body of work has appeared in a number of group and solo art shows, book covers, marketing materials, fundraising events, and public places. When she invents spare time for herself to fill, Kendra enjoys skiing, cycling, exploring, discovering new music, watching trains go by, decorating cakes with her sister, making faces in the mirror, and playing with her dog, Puck.

Photo by Amy Fesenmaier

WHEN JACK SAID "DID VELOCIRAPTOR HAVE FEATHERS?" ON PAGE 78, HE MEANT, "OF COURSE I'M SURE!" BECAUSE SOME DINOSAURS REALLY __DID__ HAVE FEATHERS. DID YOU KNOW THAT? MOST PEOPLE DON'T.